"I don't want to do something that will disrupt my daughter's life. I don't want to do anything that might get complicated."

For a moment Regan stared. Was Chase still talking about work? Or did he mean her—them?

He caressed her cheek, smoothing his thumb lightly across the skin. A soft gasp escaped her throat when he bent his head and kissed her other cheek.

Slowly he lowered his gaze to her lips, and his warm brown eyes became intent.

Then he pulled back and stared at her. She had a moment of confused hope before reality came crashing in.

Kissing him was a bad idea. A very bad idea.

She'd been attracted to Chase since they'd met, she realized now. She'd been bewildered by the feeling. Hadn't accepted it. But it had been there all along.

Now it seemed that Chase might have been fighting the same feelings.

If you're looking for fresh, sparkling and warmly emotional stories, curl up and relax with a Claire Baxter book today!

Claire is a new Australian author who writes feel-good, contemporary romances. She will sweep you away to gorgeous settings where you'll meet lovable characters.

"Claire Baxter makes a noteworthy debut with *Falling for the Frenchman,* a sweet, sensual and sometimes funny reunion tale."
—*Romantic Times BOOKreviews*

"Claire Baxter's *Best Friend…Future Wife* combines a deceptively simple plot with fabulous, multi-faceted characters. It's pure magic."
—*Romantic Times BOOKreviews*

"Claire Baxter is an author who pens stories about characters that have a history, but it's a history that will leave you spellbound."
—*www.CataRomance.com*

CLAIRE BAXTER

The Single Dad's
Patchwork Family

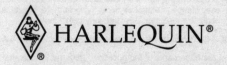

HARLEQUIN®

TORONTO • NEW YORK • LONDON
AMSTERDAM • PARIS • SYDNEY • HAMBURG
STOCKHOLM • ATHENS • TOKYO • MILAN • MADRID
PRAGUE • WARSAW • BUDAPEST • AUCKLAND

ISBN-13: 978-0-373-17509-3
ISBN-10:   0-373-17509-4

THE SINGLE DAD'S PATCHWORK FAMILY

First North American Publication 2008.

www.eHarlequin.com

Printed in U.S.A.

Like many authors, **Claire Baxter** tried several careers before finding the one she really wanted. She's worked as a PA, a translator (French), a public relations consultant and a corporate communications manager. She took a break from corporate communications to complete a degree in journalism and, more importantly, to find out whether she could write a romance novel—a childhood dream. Now she can't stop writing romance. Nor does she plan to give up her fabulous lifestyle for anything. While Claire grew up in Warwickshire, England, she now lives in the beautiful city of Adelaide in South Australia, with her husband, two sons and two dogs. When she's not writing, she's either reading or swimming in her backyard pool—another childhood dream—or even reading *in* the pool. She hasn't tried writing in the pool yet, but it could happen. Claire loves to hear from readers. If you'd like to contact her, please visit www.clairebaxter.com.

In memory of my dad (1924–2002)

CHAPTER ONE

REGAN JANTZ took a flute of champagne from a circulating waiter, then made her way to an alcove from where she scanned the mix of Japanese businessmen and local industry representatives.

'You look like you don't want to be here.'

Startled, she swung towards the deep male voice. Its owner smiled down at her. Being smiled *down* on wasn't exactly a first but it was unusual enough to make Regan give him more than a cursory glance. She hadn't realised there was someone already occupying the vantage point she'd chosen.

She pasted a professional smile on her face and at the same time took in the expensive suit, confident stance and clean-cut lines of the man's face. 'I'm sorry?'

He leaned forward and spoke softly. 'You don't look as if you're enjoying yourself.'

'Oh.' Regan stepped back. He might be tall and good-looking *and* have a nice gentle voice, but she didn't know who he was.

She saw understanding in his face and, for an instant, wished she could undo the automatic reflex. He was only trying to be friendly after all.

'I've only just got here,' she said in answer to his remark. 'I was running late.'

Glancing at her watch, she said, 'I'm hoping it won't go on too long.' She had to get home before her sons went to bed. 'But I'm sure I'll enjoy it,' she finished with a smile, just in case the handsome stranger had an involvement in the event's planning.

He took a sip from his glass and surveyed the guests filing into the function room. After a brief silence, he said, 'Do you think it's a good idea—the tourist trail?'

'Oh, yes, I do.' The enthusiasm in her tone was genuine.

The purpose of the cocktail party was to launch a new initiative of the state government's tourism department—packaging South Australia's Eyre Peninsula into an activity-filled holiday experience aimed specifically at Japanese tourists and marketed to the Japanese travel industry.

'I think it's a great idea,' she said and not just because he might have been instrumental in developing the concept.

She paused, tempted to leave it at that, but something about the keen interest in his face made her go on. Most people at these events made polite small talk and avoided showing real interest in anything.

'I'm not completely convinced that I should be getting involved with it, though.'

'Why not? What's your business?'

'I run a tuna farm.' She sipped her champagne, studying his eyes as she spoke. He had kind brown ones—not as dark as her Italian ex-husband's eyes, which both her children had inherited, but a warm reddish brown. Like the rich red-gum honey that her son Cory loved on his toast fingers.

'I can see why tourists would want to visit the seahorse farm,' she went on. 'It's a real novelty. And at the oyster farm they can sample the product, which is a treat, but when they come to visit us, well, all they'll get to do is ride out to the pontoon in a boat and see the fish in captivity. And hear us talk about the process. It doesn't compare, does it?'

'I'm sure you'll make it interesting.'

She shrugged. She wasn't so sure that was possible, but she'd do her best, of course. 'So, what about you? Why are you here?'

'I'm here on behalf of friends. They run trips for tourists at Leo Bay, taking them out to swim with the sea lions.'

She nodded, smiling. 'The trail's a perfect opportunity for them. They couldn't make it tonight?'

He lowered his voice. 'I owed them a favour. They don't like functions like this.'

'And you do?'

He gave a slight grimace. 'No. That's why I was hoping I'd found a kindred spirit when I saw you slinking over here.'

'Well, I admit it's not my favourite part of the job, but it has to be done.'

He gave her a rueful smile. 'I'm out of practice.'

'At what?'

'Small talk. With adults.'

The age lines around his eyes and mouth were just what his face needed to give it definition, she decided. Men had an unfair advantage when it came to such things.

Two vertical lines above the bridge of his nose told her he'd spent a lot of time frowning—or deep in thought. She could relate to that.

His hair too was a lighter, warmer brown than Giacomo's. Its casual style didn't go with the sharp image he presented in all other respects.

Overall, he was the most attractive man she'd seen in a

long time. Suddenly, she realised he'd stopped talking and she was still staring.

Embarrassed, she glanced away. 'Um, my main reason for coming tonight was to practise my Japanese,' she said. 'So I'd better go and mingle.'

'It was good to meet you. I'm Chase, by the way.' He held out a hand. 'Chase Mattner.'

She shook hands with men all the time; it was a necessary part of her business, and she'd experienced all sorts of handshakes from the bone-crunching squeeze to the wet lettuce leaf effect. Sliding her hand into Chase Mattner's, however, was…different.

For a split second she enjoyed the warm strength of his hand enfolding hers. Enjoyed the strange mixture of comfort and excitement that filled her.

But that was a ridiculous reaction. She didn't have time to go around enjoying handshakes and, besides, someone so attractive couldn't possibly be unattached.

Not that she wanted to know.

'Regan Jantz,' she said.

'Maybe we'll bump into each other again later.' The gleam in his eyes told her he hoped they would.

With a nod, she walked away from him. It was only then that she registered he'd said something about a lack of adult conversation. So he had children. She'd known someone so attractive couldn't be unattached. Not that it mattered. She recognised a local hotel owner and crossed the room to talk to her.

Chase watched Regan's graceful progress across the room, then looked for a waiter. There was a time when he'd have been a sucker for a blue-eyed brunette, especially one as tall and striking as Regan Jantz. But that time had long gone. He'd stopped noticing women of any type once he'd married Larissa. And since then, with everything he'd been through—losing Larissa and learning through trial and error how to raise their child alone—he'd lost the urge to notice.

Regan was lovely, though. He swapped his empty glass for a fresh one and glanced across the room to where she'd settled into a discussion with one of the overseas guests. Her beauty was in her bone structure and she'd never lose it. She was one of those women who'd become even more beautiful as she aged.

As she dipped her head to hear what the man was saying, her straight dark hair hid her face but he clearly remembered the curve of her cheek, her bright, intelligent eyes. So bright and so blue he'd thought she must be wearing coloured contacts.

Women did that nowadays, he'd heard. But once he'd started talking to her, he'd decided there was nothing fake about Regan Jantz—not the hint of auburn in her dark brown hair, not the length of her eyelashes, not even the soft pink of her lips. She was as straightforward as they came and for a moment there…

No. Not attracted. He couldn't have been attracted to her. It had been a slight tug of recognition, that was all. Recognition of the fact that she was the type of woman he *could* have been attracted to, if things had been different. Very different. In another life.

It was too soon to even say he *liked* Regan but instinct told him he could like her given the chance. She reminded him of Jan in an obscure way and he valued Jan's friendship. Jan and her husband Mike were the reason he was here tonight. In a suit.

With a shrug, he shoved his free hand into the pocket of his trousers, pushing back the jacket. He wasn't just out of practice at small talk, he was out of the habit of wearing suits and didn't even know why he kept them. They'd be out of style by the time he needed them for work again. He couldn't see himself returning to working life while Phoebe was still young enough to need him and, as she was about to turn four, that day wasn't even close.

Dragging his gaze away from Regan but reluctant to join in the general chatter, he turned to the window. The function room overlooked the Port Lincoln foreshore and, as it was still early evening, he had a panoramic view of the spectacular blue waters of Boston Bay, from the tip of Port Lincoln National Park to Point Boston. The island-dotted bay was more than three times the size of Sydney Harbour but without the big city on its shores—a fact that he guessed suited the fifteen thousand inhabitants of Australia's richest town just fine.

Port Lincoln had more millionaires per capita than any other town or city in Australia. Many of the local tuna farmers had made a packet from selling sashimi to the Japanese. He wondered if Regan was one of them.

She didn't look like a millionaire, but then he, more than anyone, should know that looks could be deceptive. His own parents were rich but they spent most of their time dressed as a pair of backpackers and avoiding the luxuries they could well afford.

They'd made it clear he was welcome to their money but could expect nothing else from them, not even their time. He didn't need their money; he had enough of his own. But he could have done with their support after Larissa's death, would have been grateful for their help with Phoebe. They'd been somewhere in Africa at the time and he hadn't seen them since.

Stifling a sigh, he warned himself not to let his thoughts go there now. He drained his glass and forced himself to face the room again. He really should follow Regan's example and mingle. Having made the trip, he owed it to Jan and Mike to represent them well.

An hour or so later, Regan found herself in the same group as Chase although they were involved in separate conversations. She wondered whether he'd engineered the coincidence. When the speeches started and all heads turned towards the small stage, he moved to her side and she tried not to feel pleased, but her nerve-endings twitched and took note of his presence.

'I think I've spoken to everybody in the room,' he said in a low voice. 'What about you? Did you get plenty of practice?'

She turned to look into his face. Hunger gripped her stomach as she did so. At least, she hoped it was hunger. If not, it was a completely inappropriate reaction. 'Practice?'

She'd meant to whisper, but she hadn't meant to sound breathless. She took in a deep breath—which didn't help since all it did was fill her nose with the clean masculine scent of Chase Mattner.

There was something about this man that threw her off her game and she didn't like it. Well, maybe she did like it, but she shouldn't.

The volume of the crowd noise had dropped further and his warm breath brushed her ear as he leaned close to whisper. 'Japanese.'

'Oh, yes. I did,' she whispered back.

He nodded, then looked towards the front of the room while she continued to study his profile, his tanned cheek, the strong line of his jaw. His lips parted slightly as he gave all his attention to the speaker. And then he laughed.

Vaguely aware of the sound of general laughter around her, she was still watching as he turned to share the joke with her, his eyes sparkling, deep creases around them...

He frowned. 'Are you okay?'

His face blurred. She tried to nod but, instead of her head, it was the room that moved. It spun one way, then the other. 'I feel...a bit...dizzy.'

Within minutes she was sitting at a table in the bar sipping iced water. She'd been aware—all too aware—of his arm supporting her on the way there, but she'd been too woozy to object. Not that she'd wanted to. Which confused her.

'Feeling better?'

She rolled her eyes. 'I'm fine. I don't know what happened.'

'You're not the fainting type, then?'

'God, no!' She was as far from the fainting type as it was possible to be. 'I've never done that before.'

'Well, it was pretty warm in there. Lots of bodies.'

'Yes.' And she'd only been aware of one. The one standing next to her. She took another sip from her glass and felt the cool water slide down her throat. She was warm, but not warm enough to explain what had just happened.

'You're not...'

She looked up when he hesitated. 'Not what?'

'You're not pregnant?'

'*No!*'

He nodded. 'It was just a thought.' His face clouded. 'I remember my wife fainting in the first few weeks of her pregnancy.'

She breathed in and out, very slowly. She'd guessed he wasn't unattached so why did the mention of his wife slice through her? It wasn't as if she cared.

'I'm definitely not pregnant.'

'What about food? Did you eat any of the finger food in there?' He gestured towards the function room they'd left.

'No. I never do eat at these things. I'm always too worried I'll get something stuck in my teeth.'

After a brief burst of laughter he stilled, watching her face. 'You're serious, aren't you?'

She nodded. She couldn't believe she'd said it out loud. What was it about this man that made her forget who she was? First she was fainting, then she was telling him her private thoughts. She was usually much better behaved.

'When did you last eat, then?'

She frowned, thinking. 'I had breakfast.'

'Nothing since then?'

'I don't think so.'

'You don't remember?'

'It's been a busy day.' She saw him look her over. She knew she was thin, but not skinny enough to cause the frown on his face.

'I do eat. It's just that I've been busy.'

'Have dinner with me.'

It didn't sound like a question.

'I can't. I have to get home. *Damn.*' She stared at her watch. It was later than she'd thought. On the rare occasions she couldn't be home in time to tuck her children into bed, she always made a point of phoning them to say good-night. But tonight she'd forgotten.

'Problem?'

'Yes. My children will be asleep by now.'

She fervently believed that all children needed to know they were loved and wanted, but when they'd already been rejected by one of the people who was supposed to love them unconditionally it was even more important to make the effort to let them know she was thinking about them. But that was the problem—she hadn't been thinking about them.

The truth made her chest heavy with guilt and she sucked in her bottom lip. She was normally so careful about things like this. She knew from experience how it felt to be forgotten by a parent. She didn't claim to be the world's best mother, but she did try to make up for being the only parent the boys had. She really tried.

'Is your husband with them?'

Her head jerked up. 'No. My mother.'

His eyebrows rose in a silent question.

'I'm divorced. My mother lives with us.' Her guilt eased a fraction. It wasn't as if they were entirely alone. Their grandmother was with them and, as Regan looked at her watch again, she knew that her boys would be fast asleep by now.

But this was the first time she'd forgotten to call them. The knot in her stomach wound tight again.

'We have something in common.' He smiled. 'We're both single parents.'

Her stomach flipped. He *was* unattached.

But she shouldn't care. She didn't need—or want—a man. Her jaw hurt. She'd been clenching it, she realised, and that was doing her no good at all. She sighed and lifted her eyes to meet Chase's understanding ones. 'I'm too late to say goodnight to my sons,' she said. 'It's the first time I haven't done it.'

He grimaced in sympathy. 'I'm sure they'll understand. Kids can be very forgiving. How old are they?'

'Will's seven and Cory is five.'

'And I have a daughter who's nearly four.' His face softened. 'Phoebe.'

She guessed *he* hadn't forgotten to phone home.

He got to his feet. 'I'd better reserve a table for us in the restaurant before they fill up.'

She opened her mouth to object, but the words wouldn't come out. Because at that moment she couldn't think of a good reason not to have dinner with him.

She nodded and watched him walk across the bar. For once she'd let someone else take the decision out of her hands, allowed someone else to take control. It felt weird, but she was a little tired of being the one who everybody came to for the answer.

Between her employees, her children and her extended family…sometimes…it was all too much.

A touch on her shoulder made her jerk, her eyes wide.

'Regan?' Chase crouched beside the chair. 'Sorry to make you jump. I couldn't get your attention. Are you sure you're feeling okay now?'

'Yes. I was just…thinking.'

He smiled and her stomach went into freefall. Oh, boy, she must be much hungrier than she'd thought.

'It's a bad habit. I'm always being told I do too much of it.' He nodded towards the restaurant. 'They have a table ready for us now.'

He rose to his feet and held out a hand. She looked at

it. If she took it, would he think she was interested in him in a romantic way? Because she wasn't.

He dropped his hand and stood back, giving her space. Part of her was glad. But, as she bent to retrieve her handbag from the floor, another part wished she'd just taken his hand. Now he'd think she was an uptight, unfriendly woman who didn't know how to act around a man.

It wasn't true but, after the experience she'd had with her ex-husband, the last thing she needed was to feel attracted to this man. Or any man.

At their table, Regan accepted a menu from the waiter with a smile. She selected the King George Whiting, a local speciality popular with tourists and for good reason. Chase ordered the same, then took the menu from her and handed it to the waiter, pushing the basket of bread rolls across the table at the same time.

'Here, have some bread while we're waiting for the fish. You need to get something inside you before you keel over again.'

She groaned and took a bread roll. 'I often miss lunch but I've never felt dizzy before. I don't think that's the reason.'

'Can you think of another one?'

She shook her head.

'Maybe you should get checked over? Go to the doctor?'

'No.' She flapped a hand. 'Total overreaction. It'll probably never happen again.' As if she'd waste her precious time in a doctor's surgery when there was nothing at all wrong with her.

She brightened. 'I know what it was…I had a glass of champagne on an empty stomach and I don't often drink.'

'That would do it.' He nodded and took a bread roll himself. 'How long have you been in tuna farming?'

'My family has been in the industry for a while. My father started the business when the quotas were cut in the late eighties. His father was a tuna boat owner and Dad inherited the boat when he died but he saw that the future of the industry was in farming, not fishing.'

'A man of vision.'

She chewed a mouthful of bread slowly and swallowed it before going on. She was proud of her dad; he'd played an integral part in establishing a whole new mentality for Port Lincoln. The major industry of the town had been in trouble when it had been completely turned around by the techniques of sea culture. Her dad and people like him had been responsible for the new industry's survival and resurgence after a couple of disasters.

Their family business was nowhere near the biggest or most lucrative, but their name was well-respected and, having reverted to her maiden name since her divorce, she intended to keep it that way.

'Never having a son of his own, Dad hoped to pass the business on to his grandsons, but he died just after my second son was born.'

'Unexpectedly?'

'Very much so.' She resisted the memories that came rushing at her. 'Heart attack,' she said in a flat voice.

'I'm sorry.'

'It was a shock at the time, but I'm over it now, of course.' She cleared her throat, which was tightening despite her statement.

'And then you took over the business?'

'No. Not right away. My husband took over.' She let her gaze slide away and over the other tables without seeing the people seated at them. 'I had a baby and a toddler so I didn't take an interest in the business. I left it to him to manage.' She snorted. 'Big mistake.'

She took a deep steadying breath. Giacomo—or, as he'd preferred her to call him, Jack—with his classical good looks and charming ways had let her down all round. It had been a tough time, and she could hardly believe she was telling this stranger about him.

Was it because she'd never see him again? Was it like talking to a fellow passenger on a plane—that sense of being able to say anything because their paths would never cross again?

Or was it because, for some strange reason, she felt a connection to him? As if he was someone she could trust. As if he was a friend.

Either way, she'd probably said enough.

'What happened?'

She turned back and met his gentle, encouraging gaze. Her resistance crumbled and the words flowed out before she could stop them.

'He had no idea what he was doing. Oh, he *talked* as if he knew all about the industry but, when it came down to it, he had no business sense whatsoever. We nearly lost everything.'

'But you found out in time to save it?'

She winced. 'I found out when he left me. Left me, his children, the business.' She spread her hands, palms up. 'The whole lot.'

She saw a flash of anger in his eyes but it was followed by concern and he waited silently for her to go on, resting his elbows on the table and his chin on his linked hands.

'That was when I took over. I didn't have a choice. Everyone depended on me. The employees. My family. I had to support my children. And I didn't know much about the business except what I'd learned from listening to Dad.' She made a frustrated gesture.

'Rather from overhearing him talk about it. He'd never tried to teach me anything because he didn't think there was any need to.' And he probably wouldn't have thought of her as a successor. Growing up, he hadn't thought about her much at all to be honest, too consumed in making the business a success. The knowledge was like a lead weight in her stomach.

She'd told Chase she hadn't a choice, but in truth she *had*. No one had forced her to take over the business. She could have let it go and found herself a job. Strictly nine-to-five.

But could she have coped with the shame of allowing the family business to be destroyed? With seeing the employees—all those people—out of a job because of her husband's bad business mistakes?

Not a chance.

She'd felt a compulsion to clear up the mess that Jack had made. She couldn't possibly let all her father's work be wasted. But that wasn't all—she'd suddenly had an irrational need to show her father she could do it. He might have been dead but Regan had still been looking for his elusive approval.

And, at the same time, she'd thought it was the best way of supporting her children. It had been a lucrative business in her father's day. If she could turn around the damage, she knew it could be lucrative again. And, when the boys were old enough, she could hand it over to them to manage. It was their heritage.

Of course, she'd underestimated how difficult it would be to juggle the demands of the business and her desire to be there for her children.

But she'd coped. Just about.

'How long ago was this?' Chase jogged her from her thoughts and she refocused on his face.

'Five years. And it's taken almost all of that time to get the business back on track.'

He nodded. 'It's going well now?'

'Touch wood.' She tapped two fingers against the dark timber table. 'Yes, it's ticking over nicely. I'm about to tie up a contract with a Japanese restaurant chain and that will set us up for several years. The pressure will be off. Finally.'

The waiter brought their meals and she leaned back while he arranged a plate in front of her. No matter how encouraging Chase was, she really should stop talking now.

'Well, I'm very impressed,' he said as the waiter left.

She made a dismissive gesture.

'No, really. What you've done is amazing.'

She could have sworn her whole body blushed. She dropped her gaze to the fish and picked up her fork. 'That's enough about me. What do you do?'

CHAPTER TWO

'So, you do nothing?' Regan looked down at the food on her plate and Chase thought he caught a flash of disapproval as she dropped her gaze.

He took a sip of water. Regan had declined wine, which was probably a good idea considering what had happened earlier, so he'd chosen mineral water, too. Technically, yes. In employment terms, he did nothing, but he wouldn't describe his lifestyle in Leo Bay like that.

Regan probably had him pegged as one of those characters the current affairs shows were keen on spotlighting. Bludgers who survived on taxpayers' money while they spent their days catching waves.

The idea of her thinking badly of him sat uncomfortably in his stomach and he hurried to explain. As she reached for her glass, he said, 'I've taken time out of my career to raise my daughter.'

Her face changed, brightened, and hell, she had a lovely smile.

'You have sole custody, too? When was your divorce?'

'I'm not divorced.' He frowned. 'My wife passed away three and a half years ago.'

After a moment's stunned silence, she said softly, 'I'm sorry.'

His head twitched in acknowledgement. He'd never got used to accepting sympathy.

'How did she…?' Flapping a hand, she said, 'No, of course you won't want to talk about it.'

'It's okay.' He paused while the waiter refilled their glasses.

He could talk about Larissa. Now. When he'd first moved from the city, he hadn't been able to. Hadn't been able to even think about her without breaking down. But that had changed. Living in Leo Bay had done that for him.

He still missed her; how could he not? They'd planned to spend a lifetime together. And he'd been happy married to her. He'd wanted the whole package—wife, kids and career.

Life had a way of ensuring a man didn't get too cocky.

Yet there were men like Regan's husband who had it all and threw it away. He felt a sudden surge of anger. He couldn't understand a man like that. He'd never know how a father could desert his children.

Life hadn't been easy for him after Larissa's death, but he'd never once thought of leaving Phoebe to someone else's care.

It had been one of his few strokes of genius when he'd decided to take a sabbatical and move out to the Eyre Peninsula beach shack that had been left to Larissa by her parents— along with a sizeable inheritance he would never touch. It would go to Phoebe when she became an adult.

Larissa had spent her childhood holidays at the shack and, though they'd never discussed it, he'd known instinctively that she'd been happy there.

From the moment he and Phoebe had arrived at the front door, he'd been filled with a sense of doing right.

It was as if he could feel Larissa's spirit all around him. As if she'd wanted them to live there. The comfort he'd taken from that odd sensation had helped to ease the pain.

It was a much more simple life he led now, away from the demands of city living and the world in general. Simple was good. It had helped him cope, helped him retain his sanity.

And then there was Phoebe. Watching his daughter grow and learn had gone a long way towards filling the hole in his battered heart.

Regan fidgeted with her napkin and he snapped back to the present. 'Cancer,' he said.

She made a sympathetic noise.

'Breast cancer. Trouble was, she found out about it the same week we learned she was pregnant and, consequently, she refused treatment and kept the bad news to herself.' He spoke matter-of-factly, but there'd been nothing straightforward about his emotions at the time he'd discovered her illness.

'By the time I worked out there was something wrong and it wasn't just the strain of pregnancy on her body that was making her sick, it was too late. It was a very aggressive disease.'

He stared at the tablecloth, tracing the white threads with his fingertip.

'I can understand what she did,' Regan said in a gentle voice.

He looked up. 'Can you?' He shook his head. 'Must be a female thing. Larissa said it was her maternal instinct. I don't believe you'd find many husbands who'd agree with that course of action.'

'No, I don't suppose so. A mother's protectiveness starts

early. Well before a baby's born.' She pulled a face. 'A father's protectiveness only kicks in after the baby's born, if…if…'

'If it kicks in at all,' he finished for her, smiling at her horrified expression.

'I'm so sorry. I wasn't referring to your situation. I didn't mean to imply you're anything like my ex.'

'No, I know.' He took another drink of water while he gathered his thoughts. 'She should have told me.' He paused, frowning. 'Don't get me wrong, I worship Phoebe and I wouldn't be without her. I wouldn't allow anything to hurt her. Anything. But to have to watch your wife die…and all the time, to know that she'd had a choice.'

He shrugged. 'She chose to die rather than live—' His voice cracked and he shook his head. He'd *thought* he could talk about that time of his life. Seemed he was wrong. 'I'm sorry.'

'No, don't apologise. It's my fault. I shouldn't have asked in the first place.' She hesitated. 'I'm so sorry about what you went through.'

He saw the truth of her words in her clear blue eyes and it warmed him. She wasn't the breezy businesswoman she pretended to be. He got the impression she had a sensitive soul.

He told her a little about his daughter while they ate, and she reciprocated by describing her two boys. Again, he wondered how her husband could have come to terms with leaving them, not to mention giving up someone as… unique as Regan. If Larissa had lived, he'd never have left her. He had no doubt about that.

Regan was telling him about her elder son's obsession with all things Roman.

'His father was from Rome originally and I suspect that Will has the wrong idea of the city—he thinks it's still like ancient Rome, full of gladiators and people in togas. I've told him it's not, but…'

'Is that where he lives now?'

She looked up. 'Jack? I have no idea where he is. Somewhere in Italy, I think.'

'You don't have any contact with him at all?'

She shook her head as she put down her cutlery. 'When he left, he just disappeared. I tried all the places I thought he might have gone, but…' She shrugged. 'He didn't want to be found, obviously. And he hasn't been in touch since. For my part, I'm glad. In fact, I consider myself lucky that I didn't have to go through a custody battle like my best friend Anna did. She had a terrible time, poor thing. At least I was spared that, but for the boys' sake…' Her face twisted.

'I can't say they miss him because they were too young when he left, but they talk to other children, so even in these days of unconventional families they know there's something missing from their lives.'

After a moment, she looked at her watch and her eyebrows shot up. 'It's late. It's time I headed home.'

'You haven't finished your meal.'

'I've had enough. I still have work to do this evening. I have this contract to sort out—the one I mentioned earlier.'

He nodded. 'I'll call a taxi and see you home.'

'No. No need. Stay and finish your meal. I have my car. It's not far and…' Her words trailed off and she looked less sure of herself.

He gave her an amused look. 'And you don't want me to know where you live?'

She winced. 'It's not you, it's…me.' She winced again at the cliché. 'I don't do this,' she said, waving a hand at her half-empty plate.

'Eat? I think we established that earlier.'

She made the gesture more expansive, encompassing the table and the two of them seated at it. 'This. When I'm not working, I'm spending quality time with my children. I don't have time for anything else.'

'You don't socialise with friends?'

She hesitated. 'Well, yes, I do. But we're not friends. We only met tonight and we'll probably never see each other again.'

He looked away. He didn't understand why he should be disappointed. Why, in one evening, she'd gone from a woman he'd admired on sight but had no intention of pursuing, to someone he was very keen to know better.

She was beautiful, but it wasn't that. Or, he should say, it wasn't *only* that. For some unknown reason, he felt comfortable with her. He could talk to her. He'd told her about Larissa and that placed her in a very select group of people.

But she wasn't interested in being his friend. She didn't even want to see him again.

Suppressing a sigh, he looked back at her, just in time to see her take a credit card from her purse.

'No,' he said, giving his hand a quick shake. 'I'm staying at this hotel. I've already charged the meal to my room.'

She put the card away. 'Thank you.'

She wasn't so pale now that she had some food inside her. She'd worried him when her face had turned as white as the tablecloth.

He wouldn't patronize her by thinking she needed—or wanted—someone to look after her. She clearly managed a successful business as well as a family all on her own, and it would be insane to imagine she was helpless, but there was something about her that made him want to help.

The slight flush in her cheeks suited her. It made her eyes sparkle more brightly, which he wouldn't have thought possible.

'Let me give you my number.' He reached into his jacket as he spoke.

'No.' She shook her head. 'Really, there's no point. I don't have time to go out. This is so unusual for me.'

He separated one business card from the small pile and held it out to her, willing her to take it. 'I don't go out either, but I'd like you to have my mobile number, just in case.'

'In case?'

He shrugged. 'In case you want someone to talk to. In case you need a friend.' He thought it sounded lame but didn't know what else to say. It just felt wrong to let Regan disappear.

She reached for the card, frowning as she scanned it. 'You're a lawyer? You didn't say so.'

'Not practising. Ignore all the details on the card except the mobile number. It's still the same.'

She nodded and slipped the card away. 'Thank you.'

He knew she had no intention of calling. She couldn't even meet his eyes. She'd probably throw the card away as soon as she got home.

It shouldn't matter. He'd only just met her. He shouldn't care whether she liked him or not.

As she stood, he pushed his chair back and got to his feet. He couldn't help it; he did care.

'Don't bother seeing me out.' She flapped a hand at him. 'I hope you enjoy what's left of your meal. And…it was nice meeting you.'

Her voice had dropped to a murmur on the last words,

but he heard her well enough to believe she meant it. Hope leapt into his chest.

'It was great to meet you, Regan.' He held out his hand and, after a slight hesitation, she shook it. 'Remember, call me if you need anything,' he said, holding on to her soft hand a second longer than strictly necessary.

She looked into his face, her eyes shining. But she didn't speak or even nod. She simply pulled her hand from his and walked away.

A week after the launch of the tourist trail, Regan rubbed her forehead and let her eyes drift away from the computer screen. She glanced across at her two sons, who were quietly colouring pictures, but she'd promised they wouldn't have to sit there for too long. They were boys; they had energy to burn.

She worked at home as much as possible in order to spend time with Will and Cory. They had an arrangement that if the boys sat quietly and let her concentrate while working at her computer, she'd reciprocate by playing a noisy game with them when she'd finished.

Regan normally had her mother around for back-up when she needed to go into the office, but her grandfather's health had taken a turn for the worse and her mother had decided to move in with him for a little while, to look after him. He'd been relatively self-sufficient till now, at least in a physical sense. Financially, he was one more person who relied on Regan. Not that she begrudged him the money. Of course she didn't.

She did wish, though, that Pop would move closer to them. He lived alone in a small town further up the coast. If he lived nearby, they'd be able to make sure he was taking care of himself. As it was, her mother would travel up to see him as often as possible and stay with him when she thought he needed some help. And Regan worried that it was too much for her mother.

With her mother at Pop's for the next week or so, she had a child-care problem. Her other back-up, her best friend Anna, was currently overseas on a long-anticipated trip to discover her roots in northern England. She missed Anna. The boys missed Anna's children, too. They were all good friends and until now she'd always been able to rely on Anna to pitch in and help when necessary.

She let out a deep sigh.

'Are you finished, Mum?'

'No, Will. A little longer.'

The boys exchanged a glance and she felt a pang. They'd sat still long enough and she wasn't achieving much anyway; she was too distracted. Closing her eyes, she wondered if any of her other friends would be able to babysit for a few hours during the next week. Unlikely. They were all busy with their own lives and, besides, she hadn't been in touch with them recently. A couple of them—girls she'd known since her schooldays—would always be friends no matter what. When they met it would be the same as always. But they lived in the city now and had their own commitments.

Other friends were married couples she'd known while with Jack. Her divorce had shifted the emphasis of those friendships and she'd felt strange with them for a while—especially when she was the odd one out in a room full of couples. In a sense, she'd been glad of the lack-of-time excuse to stay away, but she'd like to catch up with all of them again. Now, though, when she needed a favour, was not the right time.

In case you need a friend...

The memory of Chase Mattner's voice made her eyes snap open. She looked straight at the business card he'd given her. She'd intended to throw it away as soon as she'd got home from dinner that night, but something had stopped her. Instead, she'd carried it to work in her brief-case, then brought it home again and tucked it into the corner of the desk blotter in her study where it had stayed all week. And she'd thought about ringing him at least once a day.

Could she ring him?

Just to talk.

She'd been shocked at how easy it was to talk to him, to open up to him. She'd almost forgotten they'd only just met. Almost. But it wasn't every day a man like him walked into her life.

She reached for the business card with the name of a high-profile city law firm printed in a no-nonsense typeface across the top and, for the first time, read Chase's details.

Partner?

He'd been a partner? How had he managed the transition from a prestigious job like that to full-time father? And in such a place, too. She hadn't been to Leo Bay for years but, from what she remembered, there was hardly anything to the settlement—a few beach shacks, not much more. It couldn't even be called a small town.

Presumably, he didn't need to work, but didn't he want to?

Her hand shot out and pushed the card back into the spot it had occupied for a week.

What was she thinking?

She chewed on her lip. The truth was, she was think-ing it would be good to talk to him again. It would be good to see him again. It would be good to have Chase Mattner as a friend.

It had been difficult to walk away from him, but she'd reminded herself that she wasn't a great judge of men, wasn't any sort of a judge at all. Since that night, though, she'd remembered the break in his voice when he'd spoken about his wife, and the change in his eyes when he'd talked of his daughter, and she'd wished she hadn't been so emphatic about not calling.

But she'd told him she wouldn't. What would he think of her if she changed her mind now?

A little voice told her he would think nothing bad.

Her hand crept out again and she pulled the card across the blotter towards her. She could ring to thank him for dinner. She'd thanked him briefly, but it would be polite to do it again. Properly.

And what about rescuing her when she nearly fainted? If it hadn't been for him, she could have found herself sprawled across the floor of the function room and just the thought of that made her hot with embarrassment. She hadn't thanked him for saving her from the mortification of it.

She picked up the card and dug one corner into her chin while her stomach flip-flopped with indecision.

She'd do it.

As soon as she'd made the decision, her stomach cramped into a tight ball. She'd never been so worked up about a simple phone call.

Picking up the handset, she glanced across at the boys again. She couldn't talk to Chase in front of them, even if they'd have no idea who she was speaking to or what she was talking about.

'Boys, I'm just going into the next room for a minute. Don't touch anything, okay?'

She waited till they both nodded before slipping through the door into the empty dining room and dialling the mobile number on the card.

'Chase Mattner.'

Her eyes closed. Until a few moments ago, she hadn't seriously thought she'd hear his voice again and now it sent a shock right through her. It took her back to the moment he'd first spoken and her first sight of his sun-bronzed face with the kind, understanding eyes.

'Hello?' he said, his voice curious at the silence.

'It's Regan Jantz,' she said in a rush before she could change her mind and hit the disconnect button.

'Regan?'

He hadn't expected her to call. She could hear the surprise in his voice. She shouldn't have—

'Wow. I'm so glad you called.'

A shudder turned into a wave of warmth. 'You are?'

'Yes, of course. But I didn't think you would.'

'No, me neither.' Her voice sounded odd and she cleared her throat. 'Actually, I was ringing to thank you.'

'Oh?'

'For dinner.'

'You're welcome, Regan. It was my pleasure.'

'And for your help earlier that evening, for getting me out of that room without anyone noticing. I dread to think what would have happened if you hadn't been there.'

'Well, don't think about it. It didn't happen; your dignity is intact. None of your potential clients have any idea what went on.'

'Thank you.'

'No problem. I'm glad I could help.'

'I'm grateful and…' She hesitated long enough for her stomach to lurch. 'If there's anything I can do for you in return…'

There was a brief silence.

'I mean, if I can help you—'

'Well, as it happens…do you bake?'

'Bake?'

'As in cakes.'

'I used to. It's been, uh, ages. Why?'

'It's Phoebe's birthday today and she asked me to make her a pink cake for tea. Don't know why. She's never had one before so I don't know where she got the idea. But that's what she wants and I thought it would be easy.'

'You've tried to make one?'

'Uh-huh. I'm hoping you can tell me where I've gone wrong. I'm running out of time.'

An image bloomed in her mind. Chase in a kitchen. In an apron. Surrounded by baking debris. Before she knew it, a burst of laughter bubbled in her throat and she couldn't hold it back.

'I'll ignore the fact that you just laughed at me,' he said and she could hear suppressed laughter in his own voice. 'I'm desperate. This so-called cake is so bad it's not funny.'

'Right. Sorry.' She banished the picture of Chase and cleared her throat. 'What's wrong with it?'

'It's thin and crispy. Like a pizza base.'

She hissed in a breath through her teeth. 'Did you follow a recipe?'

'Yep. I borrowed a book from my friend, Jan. She's taken Phoebe for the afternoon to give me the time and space to make it. I should have asked Jan to make the cake instead.'

'But Phoebe asked *you* to make it.'

She couldn't remember the last time she'd actually *made* a birthday cake for either Will or Cory. No, that wasn't true; she could remember. It had been Will's first birthday. The only birthday Jack had been there for. Before her life had been turned upside-down. Since then, she'd resorted to shop-bought cakes. Biting her lip, she hoped the boys hadn't been disappointed. Then she rolled her eyes. They wouldn't even know the difference—but she'd make up for it. She'd make cakes for both birthdays this year. She'd surprise them with something special.

'So you see my problem.'

'Did you use all the ingredients exactly as listed?'

'Yes. It's a very old book, though. I had to convert ounces to grams.'

There was always a chance he'd made a mistake there. 'Did you open the oven door while it was cooking?'

'Ye-es. You're not supposed to?'

'It doesn't help, but look, there are lots of things that can go wrong.'

He made an exasperated sound. 'I don't suppose… you'd come and help me?'

She felt a mixture of sympathy and fear. Calling him was one thing. Going to his house was quite another. But then she thought of Phoebe coming home, expecting her pink cake. And she remembered all the cakes she'd hoped for but hadn't had during her childhood.

Her throat closed. She was close to agreeing. But could she trust herself to bake a cake after all this time? What if she messed it up?

'I don't know,' she said at last.

'It's okay, Regan. I understand. It was too much to ask.' He sighed. 'So, what do you reckon I should do?'

She was silent for a long moment. Then she heard herself suggest a solution and could hardly believe it had come from her own mouth. 'I could buy a plain cake and bring it over there and we could decorate it for Phoebe. It's a compromise but I don't think she'll care.'

'Brilliant. She won't care, but are you sure you don't mind?'

The sound of laughter reached her through the half-open door. 'Oh, there's a problem, Chase. I'll have to bring my sons with me.'

'You call that a problem? You should see my cake. No, really, it's fine. Your sons will be welcome.'

She took a deep breath. She was really going to do this. She was really going to decorate a birthday cake for a little girl she'd never met, with a man she hardly knew.

Shaking her head, she said, 'Do you have candles?'

'I…um…well, she didn't ask for them so I didn't think they were necessary.'

She smiled. 'But you have to take a photo of her blowing out the candles. She'll love it. Believe me.'

Regan wondered what had made her say that. What did she know about little girls? Except that she used to be one a long, long time ago. It felt like a long time. She *was* nearly thirty.

'Don't worry, I'll bring some. We'll be there as soon as possible.'

'Drive carefully.'

Once he'd given her directions, she hung up, then pulled the door wide. 'Boys, we're going out,' she said as she walked into the study.

A synchronized groan met her words.

'It'll be fun.' She placed a hand on Will's shoulder and ruffled Cory's dark hair. 'We're going to a place called Leo Bay. You'll like it.'

'What's there?' Will asked.

'Um, not much.'

'So why will we like it?'

'Because…' She paused. Why was she so sure they would like it? 'Because we're going to have a good time. Once I've done what I have to do, we'll go to the beach.'

Will squinted at her for a moment. 'Can we go body-boarding?'

'Sure.'

'Cool,' he said as he slid off the chair. 'Come on, Cory. Let's get the boards.'

As she ushered them both to their bedroom to change into clothes more appropriate to the beach, she spotted her mother packing a suitcase.

Regan stepped into the doorway of her mother's room. 'Nearly ready to leave?'

Her mother sighed. 'Yes. I'll be gone for a bit longer this time. I'm going to try to talk him into seeing a doctor as well.'

Regan nodded. 'Poor Pop. He thinks that seeing a doctor is the beginning of the end.'

'I know, but we have to find out what's going on. There might be a simple treatment that will prevent him getting worse.'

Her mother tucked a nightdress into the edge of the suitcase and flipped the lid closed. While she fiddled with the zip, Regan rubbed her forehead. She had to remember to take some headache tablets before leaving.

'Give him my love, won't you? And take care of yourself, too.'

Her mother nodded.

Regan went to pack a bag of her own, stuffing it with towels, sunscreen and extra clothes for Will and Cory. She would miss her mum while she was away, but Regan knew that their relationship was not a close one and never had been. She knew her mother loved her, and she adored the boys, but Regan had always been aware, growing up, that her parents were busy making the business a success. She appreciated all their hard work now, but it left her feeling a little sad at times, as if she'd missed out on something special.

Still, she was grateful for what they did have and she knew that many people had a lot less. Her mind drifted to little Phoebe, whose mother had died to give her life...

She changed into a loose dress and, after loading the boys into her car along with all the things they wanted to take, she drove to the office.

Sue, Regan's secretary, smiled at Will and Cory as she took a pile of paperwork from Regan.

'I'll be in the office next week, Sue. And I'll call you before then to make sure there are no problems.'

'Sure. So where are you all off to?' she asked. 'Looks like you're dressed for the beach.'

Cory nodded. 'Where did you say it was, Mum?'

'We're going to Leo Bay,' Regan mumbled. 'Have a good weekend, Sue.'

'You, too.'

Regan was fond of Sue but she didn't want to tell her about Chase. Sue had stuck by Regan and the business through the difficult time after Jack had left. She'd earned the right to be a little nosy and was more a friend than an employee, but Regan knew that if she even hinted that there was a new man in her life, the news that she was dating would spread through the business faster than fire through the bush.

After leaving the office, Regan went to the shops to find a plain sponge cake, bought candles, icing sugar and food colouring and then they were ready to leave.

CHAPTER THREE

REGAN only had a vague memory of a day trip to Leo Bay as a child. Her father had never taken time off work for holidays and her mother would go nowhere without him so a very limited number of day trips was all they'd managed.

The boys chattered in the back of the car and she somehow managed to answer their questions, whilst her concentration was divided between following the unfamiliar road and thinking about Chase.

This was so out of character for her, she had to wonder whether she was losing her mind. She didn't date.

But she wasn't dating, she reminded herself. She glanced at the cake resting safely on the passenger seat. She was saving a little girl from disappointment and doing a favour for a friend. That wasn't unusual, so what was the problem?

Besides, the boys would be sad if they turned back now. *They* didn't have many days out, either. Not as many as she'd like. She did her best but she had a busy schedule. She really must put aside some time for a proper holiday this year. They all deserved it.

Anyway, if she felt uncomfortable with Chase at the end of the day, she could simply walk away and never see him again. What did she have to lose?

She slowed the car as they approached a few scattered houses.

'Are we there, Mum?'

'Nearly.'

They reached the end of the road and the bay opened out before them. She braked, awed for a moment by the crescent-shaped sweep of white sand edging turquoise water. Low dunes stretched to the left and right and curved into sandy headlands at each end of the bay, enclosing and framing the perfect picture.

Recalling Chase's directions, Regan turned the car to the right and headed along the dusty road behind the dunes. Houses were built on the inland side of the road only. Chase's was the fourth and last house and had been constructed on timber posts which, Regan guessed, gave it a great view across the dunes to the ocean.

She pulled the car on to the sparse gravel frontage and stepped out of it, her eyes on the sky-blue weatherboard building. It was a beach shack, exactly as he'd said. She'd had a random thought that he might have downplayed its description and she'd find a sprawling, contemporary holiday home. But no, it was a shack, complete with paint that was peeling in places from the salt air, fishing rods on the front veranda and drifts of sand at the end of each step.

She was acutely aware that butterflies had taken up residence in her stomach, yet she did much scarier things than this all the time. This was nothing compared with her first meeting with angry, disappointed customers when she'd taken over the business. And that was only one example of what she'd learned to deal with on a daily basis. Not that she allowed customers to be let down now that she had the business under control, but still, there was always some demand on her courage.

This, though, had taken on a significance out of all proportion to what it was—a simple visit.

The boys were scrambling to get out of the car and she tore her gaze away from the house to organise them, giving Will the bag to carry and Cory the bodyboards, before reaching into the front seat for the cake. As she closed the car door, the house door opened and Chase strolled out on to the porch.

But this was a very different Chase from the one she'd encountered at the cocktail party. For an instant, she wondered if she'd have given him a second glance if he'd been in board shorts and T-shirt with bare feet when she'd met him.

But then he smiled at her and something deep inside her twisted. Was seeing a friend supposed to feel like this?

His clothes were irrelevant. It was something about *him* that made her straighten her spine and take notice, that made her nerve-endings tingle and her muscles contract.

She hadn't given a man so much as a glance since her divorce but this man had her looking.

But *look* was all she would do. And talk. He'd been so easy to talk to at dinner she'd found herself sharing information about herself she wouldn't normally give away to anybody.

Since Jack's desertion, she'd been absolutely certain that she'd never be able to trust a man again. If the one who'd loved her as deeply as she'd believed Jack had loved her could walk out of her life without a backward glance, how could she trust anybody else?

She and Jack had fallen in love the day they'd met, had been married within months, and he'd promised to love her for ever. When she'd had two babies in quick succession, she'd thought they were living the dream, that their life was picture-postcard perfect.

But while she had still been reeling from the death of her father, he'd abandoned the three of them. And not only that, but he'd left her to sort out the mess he'd created. In her book, you didn't do that to someone you loved.

It had taken her five years to dig her way out of the disaster, to get their lives back on a secure footing. Five years that had killed any love she'd ever felt for Jack, but she still thought about him. Despite their divorce, she didn't feel she'd achieved closure.

She would never again give a man the power to hurt her as Jack had done. Which meant keeping her heart under wraps and her feelings firmly under control.

Chase jogged down the steps from the veranda and crossed to where she was still standing. 'Regan, it's fantastic to see you again.' He bent to kiss her cheek.

Shock stole her voice. He'd kissed her. She wanted to lift her fingers to her cheek, to touch the blazing spot he'd brushed with his lips, but luckily she remembered she was holding the cake in time to stop her making a total fool of herself.

It was a peck, that was all. Other friends greeted her with a kiss. It was nothing out of the ordinary. She just hadn't been expecting it from him.

'Is that the cake?' He gestured at the white box in her hands.

'Oh, yes.'

'Brilliant. Thanks for doing this. Shall I take it?'

'Um…could you help Cory instead?' She tipped her head towards her youngest son, who was struggling to hold two bodyboards that were bigger than him. 'I promised I'd take the boys down to the beach afterwards.'

Chase's smile broadened to a grin and he dropped to crouch beside Cory. 'G'day, mate. I'm Chase. Can I give you a hand?'

Cory nodded.

'I've got one of these, too.'

Cory looked up at him as he straightened and tucked the boards under his arm.

'The waves here are perfect for bodyboarding.'

'Are they?'

'Yeah, not too big.'

'Cory doesn't know how to do it yet,' Will chimed in. 'Mum's tried to teach him but he keeps falling off the board.'

'Well, that's no problem. We can fix that. Shall I take the bag, Will?'

Will looked surprised that this stranger knew his name and he glanced at Regan as he handed over the bag. She gave him an encouraging smile. Will wasn't shy but he did take a while to warm up to new people.

'Remember, we have to do the cake first,' she said to her sons as they followed Chase up the steps. 'It will be a little while before we go to the beach.' Then, as she entered the cool interior, 'You have air-conditioning?'

'Yes.' Chase set the bodyboards against the wall just inside the door and moved towards the open-plan kitchen. 'It's the only change I've made to the house. Well, that and all new electrical appliances for safety's sake. I wanted to leave the decor substantially the same as when Larissa was here. It seemed right somehow.'

She nodded, looking around at the eclectic mix of furniture, the group of three sofas all covered in different fabrics, the overladen bookshelves and numerous side tables. So different from her own carefully coordinated house.

'But Phoebe was only a baby when we arrived and I was worried about her overheating.'

'That's understandable.' She placed the cake on the kitchen bench and crossed to the sink to wash her hands.

'Boys,' she called over her shoulder, 'sit quietly and play with the things you brought while we see to the cake. It won't take long.'

Chase watched them as they obediently walked to the sofa and started to take toys from the bag. 'They could play outside,' he suggested.

She shook the water from her hands and turned, holding them in front of her to dry.

'The back garden's perfectly safe.'

She nodded. 'All right.'

'Hey, guys? Can you do something for me?'

Will and Cory looked up. 'What?' Will asked warily.

'I'd like you to build something for me. Come outside and I'll show you.'

Regan watched him walk to the glass sliding doors in the back wall of the house. Will and Cory ran after him. The sight gave her a jolt. Other than Pop, who was only an occasional presence, the boys had no male role model in their lives. Most of their school teachers were women, too. Perhaps it would do them good to spend some time with Chase. Building things.

She took a breath. She mustn't get ahead of herself. She wasn't sure they'd see each other again after today.

She took another breath before opening a kitchen cabinet, looking for mixing bowls. When she had everything she needed, she emptied some of the icing sugar into the bowl and set to work.

Around ten minutes later, Chase came back into the

house. He looked from her to the bowl and back again. 'Sorry to leave you to it like that.'

'No problem. What are the boys doing?'

'Building a cubby house. I told them I've been meaning to make one for Phoebe.'

She gave him a questioning look. 'How can they make a cubby house? They're only little boys.'

He smiled. 'All boys know how to make cubbies. It's programmed into the male genes.'

'Is it safe?'

'Well, I can't guarantee they won't get a splinter, but I imagine that's the worst that will happen.'

She dropped her gaze to the bowl and swished the wooden spoon through the smooth icing. 'Sorry if I sound over-protective.' It was just that they were so important to her.

'I understand, believe me. They're safe and, if they need you, they know where you are.'

'Yes. Thank you.'

'You can see them from the window if you're worried.'

'No, no. It's fine.' She resisted the urge to cross the kitchen. She didn't want to sound like a paranoid mother. She didn't want to smother her boys, either. They needed time to do male stuff without her bobbing up to check on them.

Chase peered into the mixing bowl. 'Is this what we're going to use?'

'Yes. Wash your hands.'

He pulled a childish grimace as he walked past her to the sink. 'Yes, Mum,' he mumbled.

'I heard that.'

'You were meant to.'

She rolled her eyes at him, then grabbed a spatula and

quickly spread pink icing over the sponge cake. When Chase came to stand at her side, it was nearly finished.

'Wow. You've done it already.'

'Well, not yet. It's not finished until it looks pretty and has Phoebe's name on it.' She smoothed the last bit, then opened the piping bag and spooned the remaining pink icing into it.

'Now, watch, because I'm only going to do the first bit, then you can do the rest. You'll be able to tell Phoebe that it was your own work.'

He grinned. 'You think of everything.'

She smiled back. 'Years of practice.'

After a quick lesson and a little trial and error, Chase got the hang of piping rosettes around the perimeter of the cake and Regan left him to it while she mixed up some white icing and filled another bag. Between them, they wrote Phoebe's name in large letters, added candles, then stood back to examine their work.

'Pretty damn good, I reckon,' Chase said. 'We make a good team, don't we?'

Regan shrugged. She didn't answer his question but her stomach fluttered. She liked the sound of being on Chase's team. 'It's not bad for a rushed effort,' she said. 'I'm sure any little girl would like it.'

'Phoebe will. She'll be really happy.'

Regan looked up at the emotion in his voice. It made her swallow hard. This was how a father was supposed to feel about his child. How she'd thought Jack would feel about their boys.

Clearly, he hadn't, or how could he have left them?

She gave herself a mental shake. She had to stop thinking about Jack. She had to stop comparing Chase with him. But, even as she told herself to stop, she was thinking that she couldn't imagine Jack frowning in concentration as he did something as feminine as decorating a cake for a little girl.

Oddly, the activity hadn't diminished Chase's masculinity. Not in her eyes. Even with a blob of pink icing on his cheek. How had he managed to get it there? Without thinking, she reached up and eased it off with her finger, then popped her finger into her mouth and licked it off.

She stopped, suddenly conscious of what she'd done.

Chase's eyes were wide but, as she slowly took her finger from her mouth and dropped her hand to her side, his face creased into a smile.

'I'm not the only one,' he said. 'You have some on your nose. Can I lick it off?'

Her hand flew to her nose but she could feel no icing. She peered at her reflection in the microwave door. 'I do not.'

'Made you look.'

She gave him a mock glare but all he did was laugh and she joined in.

'I'll clean up here, then make us a coffee. Why don't you go and see how your sons are doing?'

She looked around at the messy kitchen. 'I'd better help you clean up.' She reached for an empty mixing bowl but he caught her wrist.

She held her breath, concentrating on the contact between their skin but if he noticed the heat it generated, he didn't let on. He turned her till she faced in the opposite direction. 'I'm quite capable of cleaning my own kitchen. You've done enough.' Giving her a little push, he said, 'Go and see your boys. I know you want to.'

* * *

'Mummy!'

Chase heard the excited shout as Regan slid open the door, then the sound died as she closed it behind her.

He smiled as he started to stack bowls and utensils in the dishwasher. Regan was clearly a devoted mother. He knew better than anyone that being a single parent was a difficult job, and Regan had juggled it with the responsibility of running a business. That had to be hard. He didn't think he could have done it.

As he added powder to the dishwasher and closed it, he caught sight of the cake and thought again that it looked great. He couldn't imagine what he would have ended up with if Regan hadn't phoned at that moment. He could hardly believe she had. It was…fate.

He winced at the fanciful idea, but he'd have laid significant money on the certainty that she'd never use the number he'd given her.

He was lucky she was the type of person to care about his predicament. She could have been unsympathetic and brushed him off with an excuse, but no, she'd come to his rescue. She had a kind, warm heart under the businesslike exterior. He'd suspected as much.

The cake aside, he was thrilled that she'd called. It was great to see her again, especially in her summery dress. It wasn't particularly revealing but it was much better than the shapeless suit she'd worn at the launch party. She looked gorgeous.

A pang of guilt stopped him as he reached for a cloth to wipe down the kitchen bench. Hand poised, he realised he hadn't thought about Larissa all afternoon. Other than a brief mention when Regan first arrived, he'd relegated her memory to the back of his mind.

How had he managed that? Maybe if Phoebe, his little

carbon copy had been there, reminding him with every facial expression and every gesture…

Grabbing the cloth and turning on the tap, he told himself not to go there. He wasn't being unfaithful to Larissa's memory by having Regan visit. The only reason he hadn't thought about her was that they'd been busy. They'd been up against a deadline. He hadn't had time to indulge in memories.

While he dried his hands before making the coffee, he glanced out of the window and paused when he saw nobody. But, as he watched, Regan's face appeared in the gap between the stacked plastic crates which he assumed to be the doorway to the cubby. She grinned as she quickly crawled out, then laughed as Cory chased her around the half-built cubby. He laughed, too, though she couldn't hear him. It felt good to see her in high spirits. He got the impression she was at her happiest when spending time with her sons. He was surprised by a wave of warmth towards the little family he'd just met and a wish that he could make them all happy, all the time. He shook his head at the crazy thought and went about making the coffee.

A few minutes later, after placing two mugs on the veranda table, he carried two small cartons of juice over to the construction site.

'Drinks time,' he called.

Will and Cory popped up in front of him and took the cartons with polite thanks.

Regan made her way more slowly to his side. 'Haven't they done a great job?' she said, her eyes sparkling.

'Wonderful. Better than I could have done.'

She gave him a grateful smile. In the sea breeze, her loose skirt slapped against her legs, revealing their long, slim shape. Before he'd had time to take in the view, she'd grabbed the fabric and shaken it loose.

'Coffee's ready,' he said, jerking his head towards the veranda.

'Thanks.'

They turned together and walked to the table. He waited for her to slide on to the bench on one side, then sat opposite.

'Did you manage to stitch up the Japanese contract you were working on last week?'

'Yes.' She sighed. 'I'm glad that's settled.'

'So what goals do you have for the business now? More contracts? Or do you need to increase production before you can sell more? Which comes first?'

'I do want to expand at some stage, but not yet. For now, my main goal is stability. I want to consolidate the strong position we're in now that we have the restaurant contract.'

He watched her take a sip of coffee. Today she had her hair pulled back from her face and held by a clip at the back of her head. It meant there was no hair around her face to distract his attention from her eyes, and they seemed even larger. Incredibly beautiful eyes.

He lifted his own coffee mug in an effort to pull his gaze away. 'What about life outside work?'

'Same goal. Stability.' She smiled. 'Outside work, the boys are my life—making sure they have everything they need, keeping them safe and happy. I don't have time for anything else.'

She avoided his eyes. He wondered if she thought he wanted more than friendship from her. He'd have to make it clear that he didn't. He wanted no confusion between them.

'What do you do to relax?' he asked.

'Relax? What's that?' She laughed. 'I do play a mean

hand of snap. And I'm pretty good with a cricket bat, although I can't bowl or catch a ball.'

'Do you ever do nothing? To recharge your batteries?'

'I believe that's what sleep was designed for.'

He took another mouthful of coffee while she looked towards the boys.

'What did you do before you were married?' he asked.

She looked at him and frowned as if she was dragging up a distant memory. 'I was doing media studies at university. To be honest, I had no real ambition to go into media; I just chose that course for something to do. Studying film sounded like fun.' She had a wistful look.

'Did you finish the course?'

She shook her head. 'I was home for the summer holidays when Jack arrived in town. He was sailing around the world with a family friend and, along with a group of my friends, I was invited to a party on board their yacht. We met. He didn't go any further on his trip and I didn't go back to uni.'

Chase lifted his eyebrows. 'Love at first sight?'

She caught her lower lip between her teeth before nodding.

'So, how long had you known each other when you were married?'

'Not long at all. A few months. He had dual-citizenship because his mother was born in Australia so we didn't even have to wait for a visa. We got married and, before I knew it, I was pregnant with Will.

'I know what you're getting at but, the thing is…' She looked at the table, hunching her shoulders as if she were physically grappling with emotion. 'I don't think we were married too soon. That's not why we're divorced. We were definitely in love when we got married.'

'And when he left?'

She looked up and their eyes locked. 'I thought we were still in love. That's what hurt.'

'Oh, Regan.'

'He didn't have to leave. If he'd admitted that he didn't know what he was doing with the business, we could have worked it out between us. But he took the coward's way out. He ran away.'

Her eyes filled up and, instinctively, he reached for her hand but, before he'd touched it, a sudden noise made him turn towards the house. The door slid open and Phoebe emerged, running towards him with her arms out wide.

CHAPTER FOUR

REGAN blinked away the tears that had threatened to fall and turned to see a little girl with brick-red hair run from the house. She stopped before she reached Chase, her attention caught by Will and Cory under the tree. She changed direction and walked to within a short distance of them, then stood with her head tilted.

'What are you doing?'

Will left the cubby and stood facing her. 'Are you Phoebe?'

She nodded. 'Who are you?'

'I'm Will and that's Cory.' He pointed at his brother, who was still on his knees. 'We're making this cubby for you. Your dad asked us to.'

Phoebe gasped. 'Can I see?'

When Will nodded, she ran forward and all three of them disappeared inside the unfinished building.

Chase winked at Regan. 'That was easy.'

Before Regan had responded, a woman appeared in the doorway. Mid-thirties at a guess, Regan thought. Average height, short blonde hair tucked behind her ears and deeply tanned skin.

'There you are.' Her eyes rested on Regan for a

moment, then, with a questioning glance at Chase, she approached the table.

'Jan, this is Regan. She's saved my life today.'

Regan got to her feet and held out a hand to the other woman. Jan took it and Regan felt she couldn't have undergone a more thorough examination if she'd been an exhibit in a museum.

Finally, Jan let go of her hand and lifted the corner of the cloth covering the plate in her other hand. 'Glad you're here. You can help us eat all this fairy bread that Phoebe talked me into making for her birthday tea.' She broke into a smile.

Chase smiled at Jan, then at Regan. 'Jan and her husband, Mike, are the friends I represented at the cocktail party.'

Regan nodded. She knew Jan was half of a couple but she was also Chase's friend and had been for much, much longer than she had. Jan had prior claim and was probably wondering what she was doing there. 'Um, I wasn't actually planning to stay for tea.'

'Oh, you must,' Jan said.

'Please,' Chase added.

'I said I'd take the boys down to the beach once I'd finished with the cake.' She glanced at her half-empty mug. 'So, when I've finished my coffee, we'll leave you in peace.'

'But I offered to help Cory with his bodyboarding skills,' Chase pointed out.

She shook her head. 'I don't expect you to do that.' She hadn't thought he meant it at the time. She certainly wasn't going to hold him to it.

He frowned. 'But Cory does.'

'He'll understand.' She didn't want to think about her

sons being disappointed. She'd have to take care how she worded the news. She took a long drink of coffee. When she put down the mug, both Chase and Jan were frowning at her.

'I don't understand,' Chase said. 'The kids are getting on well. After tea we can all go to the beach and you won't have to worry about feeding the boys when you get home.'

She drew in a breath. 'That's true.'

'Please stay. I'd like you to get to know Phoebe a little, see what she thinks of the cake.'

'I'm sure she'll love it.'

Jan gave her a kind look. 'If you think you might be intruding, don't. We'll be pleased to have you stay.'

'No,' she said hastily. She felt blood rush to her face, embarrassed that she was so easy to read. 'Okay, thanks. We'll stay for tea.'

'Good.' Chase pushed back his chair as he got to his feet. 'I'd better make something besides fairy bread, then.'

'We'll give you a hand,' Jan said. 'Won't we, Regan?'

'Sure.'

Jan moved to her side as she stood. 'Glad you decided to stay.' She nodded at Chase's back as he disappeared inside. 'This self-imposed isolation isn't good for him.'

'It's easy to understand, though, given what he's been through.'

Jan nodded. 'But his wife's been dead more than three years. He needs to start living again.'

Regan dropped her gaze. 'I guess he will in his own time.'

They'd moved forward slowly and Jan stood aside to let her enter the house. 'Great to see Phoebe playing with your boys.'

Regan glanced over her shoulder. Yes, it was. Not only for Phoebe's sake but for theirs, too. They were missing their regular playmates. It would be good for them to have another child around.

Once she entered the house, she had no time to think. Jan appeared to be very familiar with Chase's kitchen and took charge, doling out tasks to the two of them as if it was her home, her daughter's birthday tea. But Chase didn't seem to mind.

Regan found herself next to him as she chopped a melon for a fruit platter and he spread bread for the sandwich fillings Jan was preparing.

His face creased as he smiled down at her. 'Jan did a stint in the army when she was younger,' he said softly.

'It shows.'

'Will Mike be joining us?' he asked over his shoulder in a louder voice.

'No, I told you.' Jan crossed the kitchen, wiping her hands on a towel. 'He's busy.' She grabbed a pile of small plates and headed outside.

Regan fidgeted with the knife she held. 'Perhaps I should go home.'

Chase put down his butter knife and reached out to touch her arm. 'I thought you'd decided to stay?'

It was a purely instinctive gesture but, the second his fingers made contact, she felt comfort flowing from them. It was disconcerting that he could have such an effect on her with the lightest touch. When he began to move his fingers in small up-and-down strokes it wasn't comfort that made her tingle in odd places.

'What's the problem?'

She made a mental grab for normality. 'People might get the wrong idea. About us.'

'Who? Jan?' He shook his head. 'What does it matter,

anyway? We're the only people who have a say. As far as I'm concerned, I'm glad I went to the launch of the trail. I'm glad I met you, Regan. I think we're going to be good friends.'

She sucked in a breath, his words seeping in through her pores and feeling…great.

'But you didn't need me to tell you that, did you?'

Actually, she did. It was exactly what she'd needed. It was a relief to know he wanted the same as her. To be friends. Good friends, but no more and no less. She broke into a smile.

'Stay?'

Their eyes met and she felt a strange reaction in her stomach, an indescribable tug. The moment stretched. Neither of them seemed able to look away. At last, the sliding door opened and Regan forced herself to turn, to go back to slicing melon. She hadn't answered his question, she realised.

'Bread ready?' Jan asked as she entered the kitchen.

'Yes.' Chase moved aside to show his handiwork.

'What about the fruit?'

'Almost done,' Regan answered without looking round.

'Good. I hope your boys are hungry.'

'Oh, I'm sure they'll eat their full share.'

She grinned at Chase who, on his way to the fridge, grinned back at her over Jan's head. She was happy she'd decided to stay and she could see he was happy, too.

Some time later, with the three adults and three children sitting around the veranda table eating cake and talking loudly, Regan tried to remember when she'd laughed so much. Much of the laughter had been provoked by Will and Cory. She'd known Will was good at impressions but had thought he'd only ever do them for her and Cory, believing him too shy to perform in public. Proving her wrong, he'd entertained them all with accurate renditions of cartoon characters.

And Cory…well, he was just a natural comic. He'd had them roaring at facial expressions alone. A knot of emotion tightened her throat. These were her boys and she was so proud of them. She loved them deeply and she'd never let anything hurt them.

Nor anyone.

She'd never put them in a position where they could be rejected again. Where another man could walk out like Jack had.

Chase caught her attention. 'Where were you?'

She shrugged. 'Daydreaming.'

'Didn't look like a happy daydream.'

'No.' She gave him a smile. 'But I am happy, here and now.'

He nodded and, from the look in his eyes, he knew exactly what she meant. And she supposed he did, although Chase's regrets would be very different from hers. While she wished she could have been a full-time mother as she'd intended, he'd devoted years to his daughter. He'd given up a high-flying job in order to give her his full attention. Perhaps he'd missed the work, but at least he hadn't missed any of the milestones, nor the first-time experiences.

For a second she envied him, but then she gave herself a mental shake. The man had lost his wife in tragic circumstances. How could she possibly consider him lucky? Her life could have been worse. Jack could have taken the boys with him or plunged her into years of custody battles. At least she'd had them with her. It had been hard to cope sometimes, but at least she'd had the joy of their company.

She watched Chase teasing Will. She'd never known Will take to anyone the way he'd accepted Chase. In one afternoon he'd put both boys at their ease, made them trust him.

'Are we going to play cricket, Daddy?' Phoebe asked.

'Well, is the sky blue?'

'Yes,' she said, giggling.

'Then of course we're going to play cricket. We have to take advantage of having all these extra players.'

Chase smiled across the table at his daughter and Regan's heart squeezed. So much love in that smile.

'After that, we'll have a swim and I'll help the boys with their bodyboarding skills.'

'Yay!' Will and Cory looked thrilled by the prospect.

'And you can swim with Regan. How's that, Sweetpea?'

Phoebe grinned across at her, but Regan spluttered. 'Oh, no, I…' She faltered at Phoebe's puzzled expression, but the thought of Chase seeing her in a swimsuit made her cringe. Especially her badly fitting old suit that she'd had for years. The horror of it. She turned to him. 'There's no need for both of us to get wet. I'll watch from the shore.'

'Well, I hoped you'd look after Phoebe for me,' Chase said, 'and nothing will keep her out of the water. You don't mind, do you?'

Regan exhaled slowly. How could she refuse to look after his daughter while he was giving his time to her sons? She couldn't. She would just have to grin and, hopefully, not bare it. 'No, of course I don't,' she said, turning on a smile for the little girl.

Later, Regan stood waist-deep in the ocean while Phoebe played around her. The water was so clear she could see her own feet and the schools of small fish that approached, then turned and fled, startled by Phoebe's splashes.

Self-consciously, she pulled the front of the swimsuit higher on her chest, but that only caused it to ride up at the bottom, exposing more than she considered decent. At least her lower half was underwater.

Even as a teenager she'd had difficulty finding swimsuits that were long enough for her body but, considering this one was years old and the elastic was past its best, it was impossible to be anything but self-conscious. It had never been an issue before. She'd taken the boys swimming loads of times but there'd never been anyone around who she wanted to impress.

She stumbled over the thought. Why exactly did she want to impress Chase? If they were only ever going to be friends, and they'd already agreed that they were, it didn't matter what she looked like.

At the sound of Will's laughter, she looked over to where the boys—all three of them—were riding the moderate waves. Cory had got the hang of it pretty quickly with Chase's expert help and they all appeared to be having a great time. Even Chase.

It came as no surprise that Chase had a fantastic body. Even fully clothed she'd got that impression. But the bubbling heat that erupted when she looked at him *was* a surprise. She hadn't felt anything like it for a long, long time and she guessed that was why she was anxious to be seen in her best light.

Oh, well, she'd just have to get over it. He'd seen her at her worst now so it was too late to care, and it wasn't as if she was going to continue having inappropriate thoughts about her *friend*. She planned to stop right now.

Without warning, Phoebe launched herself at Regan, then scrambled up her body, wrapping her legs around Regan's waist and hanging on to one of the swimsuit straps.

Regan's arms automatically went around the little girl to hold her in place. 'Had enough swimming now?'

Phoebe nodded, then snuggled her head into the curve of Regan's shoulder. Regan stroked back the wet hair that clung in strands to Phoebe's cheek, conscious that it had been a while since she'd last held one of her boys like this. They were growing up so quickly. She'd have to coax lots more cuddles from them before it was too late, before they were too old for them.

'We'd better get you home,' she said softly.

Phoebe closed her eyes in response and Regan smiled as she began to wade towards the others. Chase came to meet her.

'We have a tired little girl here,' she said.

He gazed at his daughter and held out his hands. 'I'll take her.'

'No, it's okay. Don't disturb her.'

'Are you sure?'

She nodded.

'Well, thanks. Let me know if she gets too heavy for you.' He waded back to the boys and she heard their groans as he told them the fun was over. A pang of guilt hit her in the chest. They'd probably never had such a fun-filled day in their lives. She did her best, but she was only their mum. She wasn't adept at sports. This was the stuff their father should have done with them.

A sigh ripped out of her before she moved towards the beach. Seriously, though, she couldn't imagine Jack body-boarding. Even if he hadn't left, she doubted he would have enjoyed this sort of leisure activity. Sailing, yes—she could see him taking the boys out on a flashy yacht—but not sharing simple pleasures. He just wasn't the type.

Chase regarded the boys, curled at each end of the sofa, asleep, and wondered what Regan would say when she finally appeared from the bathroom. He knew she intended to leave immediately, but while she'd been in the shower and he'd been putting Phoebe to bed, the boys had half-dressed themselves and flaked out. Personally, he thought it would be a good idea to put off leaving till the next morning.

Not that he had any ulterior motive for wanting her to stay.

He clenched his jaw for a moment. He'd known she was beautiful, but when he'd first seen her in her skimpy swimsuit, shock had rippled through him. Shock and awareness.

Those long limbs accounted for the graceful way she moved—with the elegance of a catwalk model but without the conscious effort. The slim hips and sleek muscles had nearly turned him inside out.

To experience such a strong physical reaction to the sight of her had come as a complete surprise to him.

He'd found it difficult not to see her breasts. He'd tried not to. He didn't want to *want* her. But if it hadn't been for the distraction of Will and Cory, he wouldn't have been able to keep his eyes off her.

Larissa had been gone for over three years. He had no reason to feel guilty for the enjoyment of staring at a woman's body. But he *did* feel guilty. He did feel as if he were being unfaithful. He was shocked that his hormones could lead him into betraying Larissa's memory.

He supposed that, after so long, it was only natural to

have those feelings. Even Larissa would have said they were a normal reflex.

He shook his head. This was no time to be having such thoughts about Larissa. No matter what faults she'd had as a wife, he'd loved her. And, as for his feelings towards Regan, they were entirely inappropriate.

He was lucky that Jan didn't know about his reaction to Regan. She'd been making the point for months that *he* was still alive and should get out and meet women. She'd scoffed at his insistence that the desire had died with Larissa. He'd be treated to a major dose of told-you-so if she had any idea how affected he'd been. So he'd make sure she didn't find out. He'd be careful to hide his response in future. He'd been unprepared, that was all.

He didn't want to be attracted to Regan. That would complicate his life and he didn't do complicated. He'd found, since Larissa's death, that he needed life to be straightforward and simple in order to cope with it.

He heard the bathroom lock slide back and turned expectantly. As soon as she appeared in the doorway, he put a finger to his lips and tilted his head towards the sofa. With a small frown Regan walked around the furniture until she stood next to him.

He didn't own a hairdryer so she'd combed her wet hair straight back from her face and tucked it behind her ears. He could see a pulse beating in her temple and faint lines fanning out from the corners of her eyes. The stark style made her seem more vulnerable.

Or was that just his imagination?

She sighed. 'Could you give me a hand to get them into the car?'

He waited a second, then said, 'It's the weekend tomorrow. If you don't have an urgent reason to rush back, why don't you all stay here tonight?'

Her eyebrows shot up. 'We couldn't put you out like that.'

'It wouldn't put us out. Phoebe and I would enjoy it.'

She looked away. He guessed she was going to say she had to get home, that she had work to do.

'Where would we sleep?' she asked, surprising him. 'You don't have many rooms.'

He glanced down at her sleeping sons. 'What about boys in one room, girls in the other? Phoebe has a double bed; you could sleep in there with her. Or, if you don't want to share, you put some sofa cushions on the floor in her room. Then again, I'm sure we could borrow an inflatable bed from Mike and Jan; they have heaps of camping gear. It's a simple problem to fix, Regan. Multiple options.'

She licked her lips and he found himself watching the trail of moisture her tongue left behind. Something stirred deep inside him. He chose to ignore it.

'The boys might be frightened when they wake up in unfamiliar surroundings.'

He just looked at her.

She gave him a crooked smile. 'That was an over-protective mother speaking, wasn't it? I probably sound ungrateful, but I'm not. Really. It's just that I'm used to doing things according to plan. My life is so busy, I have to plan and prepare or I can't cope. But you're right. It would be much simpler to stay. So thanks, we will.'

By the time they'd settled the boys in his room on a double inflatable mattress that Chase had borrowed from Jan, Regan wondered what they were going to do all evening. Just the two of them. She hadn't been alone with a man for years. And this wasn't like sharing a table for two in a busy restaurant. Nor was it like working together in the kitchen with the boys close by. It was intimate. Hours with only each other for company.

She couldn't see Chase when she closed the door to the passageway. Then she heard the squeak of a cork being pulled from a wine bottle and found him in the kitchen.

He smiled. 'I usually sit on the front veranda with a cold beer and watch the sun go down over the sea. Thought I'd open some wine tonight.'

'That sounds like a nice idea, but I don't think I should drink. After what happened last week…'

'You've eaten today so you'll be safe. Trust me.'

She looked deep into his eyes. A part of her wanted to trust him. With her friendship. She'd been drawn to him from the first moment she'd seen him. She felt as if they were meant to meet. Meant to be friends.

Nodding, she said, 'I do. I trust you.'

His smile was almost triumphant as he filled a glass for her. 'Come on, let's head outside.'

CHAPTER FIVE

REGAN sipped the wine and let the fresh, fruity flavour slide over her tongue, enjoying the soft lingering acidity. It had been a long time since she'd had wine just for the sake of it. She'd forgotten how nice it could be.

'It's been a good day,' she said as Chase sat beside her. 'Cory has learned a new skill, you've got out of making a cubby house, and Phoebe loved her cake.'

'Yes.' He grinned. 'God knows what she'll ask for next year. You can expect a frantic phone call.'

A year. She couldn't think that far ahead. She cleared her throat. 'Does Phoebe look like her mother?'

Chase's grin faded. 'Yes, she does. I imagine when she grows up she'll be exactly as Larissa was when I met her. Petite and perfect.'

Regan felt a spear of pain in her chest.

Why?

Why should it matter that he liked his women small?

Why would she even consider herself in competition with his dead wife?

Because she wasn't.

Annoyed with herself, she squared her shoulders and lifted the glass to her lips. After a slow drink, she glanced sideways. Chase was gazing into the distance. At a guess, he wasn't seeing the haunting yellow glow of the setting sun but was haunted by a very different picture. One that featured his wife.

Her throat thickening, she searched for something to say to ease his pain, but then he spoke again.

'Larissa saved my life.'

Regan gasped.

'Not literally. She didn't drag me out of a burning building or take a bullet for me. Nothing so dramatic. It's just that my life was one of excess until I met her. You know the sort of thing. I had too much money and I wasted it on drinking too hard, driving too fast...the usual misspent youth.'

She nodded. Not that she'd ever done any of those things. She'd been far too uptight...

Now where had that thought come from?

She'd been careful, yes. Wise for her years, even. She'd always been a deep thinker. A planner. But uptight was Jack's word—one he'd used during their rows. Because, as much as they'd been in love, they'd disagreed on so many things.

Shaking off the memory, she refocused on Chase. This was about him. Not her. 'She stopped you doing those things?'

'Exactly. Just meeting her was enough to stop me. She was so full of life. So bubbly and vivacious. Happy-go-lucky, I suppose. She didn't take life too seriously, and she made me realise there were better things to do with my time than try to kill myself through over-indulgence.'

Regan couldn't help making the comparison with herself. As much as she knew she shouldn't, she couldn't help thinking that Larissa had been her complete opposite.

Oh, she enjoyed herself with the boys, of course, but she was hardly the life and soul of the party. She never *went* to parties. She did take things seriously; she always had.

'I sometimes wonder…' He slid a glance sideways and she gave him a nod of encouragement. 'I sometimes wonder whether I should have insisted on her having treatment. I wonder whether I let her down by standing by helplessly and allowing her to die.'

'That decision was hers alone. And I'm sure it wasn't an easy decision for her to make.'

He nodded but his expression was closed. She ached for him. Even after three years, he was clearly still struggling with grief, guilt and all the other emotions a man in his position had to feel.

'Phoebe seems very affectionate,' she said in an effort to lighten the mood.

'Oh, she is.' His face brightened. 'But in a different way. She's not as open as Larissa. She's more cautious with her affection.'

'That could be a good thing,' she suggested.

'True. I'm glad she's taken to you.'

Regan blinked at him. 'You think she has?'

'Definitely. She wouldn't let Jan carry her for ages.'

Warmth tingled in Regan's tummy. She'd found Phoebe to be very open. In fact, she'd considered herself the more reserved of the two. Maybe it was the excitement of her birthday.

'Well, it's mutual. I've taken to her, too.' She smiled, remembering the way Phoebe had snuggled into her as she'd fallen asleep.

Chase's eyes gleamed approval in the golden twilight and Regan felt herself sinking. Being attracted to Chase was like walking on quicksand. She wanted to resist; she'd had every intention of resisting, but still, she couldn't help being sucked under.

Trembling, she drained the last drop of wine and stared into her empty glass.

'How do you feel?'

Her breath caught in her throat and she lifted her eyes warily. 'What?'

'The wine. It wasn't too much? You're not going to pass out?'

'No.' With a relieved chuckle she said, 'In fact, I'd like another one, if you don't mind.'

'Not at all.' He refilled both glasses. 'You were right, it has been a good day. I feel like celebrating.' He smiled as he passed her glass back to her. 'Are Will and Cory like their father?'

'In looks, yes. They both have his olive complexion, his black hair and eyes.' She sipped while she squinted thoughtfully. 'But I can't say I've seen any evidence of Jack's personality in either of them.'

Chase twisted towards her and leaned an elbow on the back of the bench. 'You sound relieved. There must have been something good about him or you wouldn't have fallen in love with him in the first place.'

'I thought there was.' She turned away and contemplated the deepening colours of the sky. Yellow had become orange with bands of crimson. Odd shafts of sunlight speared into the sky like searchlight beams. 'You watch this show every night?'

'It's a ritual. After Phoebe goes to bed, I sit out here till it gets dark.'

'Doing nothing?'

There was a slight pause before he said, 'Doing nothing. You should try it some time.'

She lifted one shoulder in a half-shrug. 'That's what I'm doing. I'm here when, in fact, I should be checking my emails. That's what I normally do when the boys have gone to bed.' She rolled her head to the side. 'Don't you miss work at all?'

'Yes, of course I do.'

'What type of lawyer were you?'

'An honest one?' He flashed a grin, then became serious. 'Corporate. I was responsible for pulling together mergers and acquisitions, giving general corporate advice. I miss the challenge of it. That's not to say that raising Phoebe isn't a challenge, too, but you know what I mean.'

He pulled a face. 'I don't think I realised till I had dinner with you last week how starved I was for adult conversation. Nothing against Mike and Jan, it's just that Phoebe's usually the centre of attention when we're together, and rightly so.'

During the birthday tea it had been obvious that Jan cared about Chase, in a platonic way. Almost as if they were brother and sister. Regan had felt herself under scrutiny, but she hadn't resented it. Chase was lucky to have such good friends to look out for him. Friends who were there to help at a moment's notice.

She took a drink and let her head drop back against the bench. The searchlight beams had gone now that the sun had sunk lower, and purple had joined the other colours painted across the sky. It was so spectacular, she wanted to do nothing but watch. Which was all she had to do.

* * *

Chase saw Regan's head nod forward on to her chest and moved quickly to take the not-quite-empty glass from her slack fingers. He couldn't leave her in such an uncomfortable position so he shuffled closer and, sliding an arm around her shoulders, supported her head with his own shoulder.

As soon as he'd settled her there, he recognised the smell of apple-scented shampoo. He knew the scent well; it was the shampoo he used on Phoebe's hair. He'd told Regan to help herself and he was glad she'd done so, but it felt odd. The familiar fragrance triggered a protective feeling for this grown woman that was normally reserved for his daughter.

He had no right to feel protective towards her.

Even with his wife he'd had to stifle this side of himself. Larissa would have none of it, even when it had come to a matter of life and death.

And Regan, he guessed, would be horrified.

He was intrigued by Regan. She was a complex mix of competence and vulnerability. He admired her for what she'd done in turning around the family business. It must have taken guts and determination and more than a little ability to accomplish.

But it was her softer, vulnerable, caring side that had such an impact on his senses. That made him want to fight her battles for her. He'd never been violent but if he had a few minutes alone with her ex-husband…

Regan was as different from Larissa as it was possible to be. Whereas Larissa was fun-loving and fearless, Regan was more serious, although she didn't lack a sense of humour, and he had the impression she'd had to face down her fears to achieve what she had.

And Larissa, he had to admit, had always been slightly

self-centred, fun but focused on her own enjoyment. Regan seemed more concerned about other people.

He took a deep breath and filled his nostrils with the scent again, registering that there was a subtle but very real difference. Apple shampoo mingled and combined with the smell of warm skin.

The warm skin of a beautiful woman.

It was a definite turn-on and his instinctive response shook him.

Her hair had fallen across her face and he stroked it back with a light touch. It was dry now and silky-smooth. He itched to slip his fingers in deeper, lift it away from her scalp and let it slide back through his fingers.

A shudder rippled through him at the imagined sensation.

It seemed he had no choice when it came to having inappropriate thoughts about Regan. But he didn't have to act on them, and he wouldn't. Instead he tried to call up a memory of holding Larissa in this way, but all that would come was a sense of emptiness and need.

Giving up, he deliberately blanked his mind and settled back to wait for Regan to wake. He could feel the movement of her breathing against his chest and he focused on its rhythm as the sky grew dark around them.

An hour or so later, Chase accepted that this was no brief doze. Far from showing signs of waking, Regan had relaxed heavily against him, her breathing deep and regular.

He could see no choice but to carry her to bed. He could hardly leave her to lie on the bench and it seemed mean to rouse her from a deep sleep that she clearly needed.

He reached forward to hook his right arm beneath her knees and swept her up as he got to his feet. For all her height, she was very light.

Nudging open the door to Phoebe's room with his

shoulder, his heart swelled, as always, at the sight of the little girl sleeping with her teddy in her arms—the toy that Larissa had kept from her own childhood.

He managed to ease Regan beneath the covers on the other side of the bed without waking either of them. It was a pity Regan had to sleep in her dress, but there was no way he was going to remove her clothes. That would well and truly overstep the boundaries of their friendship. For the same reason, he resisted the urge to drop a kiss on to her lips, and backed out of the room, closing the door softly.

It didn't take him long to tidy the house; it had become routine after all this time and he knew he had to do it before bed or it would seem overwhelming in the morning. He wasn't a natural homemaker. It was a skill he'd had to acquire. And he'd learned early on that a simple, uncomplicated routine was best for both him and his daughter. It was how he'd survived the single life and stayed sane.

Regan's eyes flew open and she sucked in a sharp breath. Then she heard a giggle and Phoebe appeared in her line of vision. So that was what had woken her.

She took in her surroundings. She was in Phoebe's bed but the last thing she remembered was watching the sunset with Chase. She'd felt relaxed and sleepy.

Embarrassment swept over her and she groaned. She must have fallen asleep in front of Chase and…he must have carried her to bed.

Hearing Regan's groan, Phoebe swung around and knelt beside her. 'You're in my bed.'

She made an effort to act as if this was nothing unusual. 'I know, sweetie, and I had a lovely sleep. What about you?'

She nodded. 'This is my teddy.'

'Oh, wow. Isn't he cute?'

'*She.*'

'Sorry. Isn't *she* cute?'

'She was my mum's teddy. Did you know my mum?'

Regan was saved from answering by a knock on the door. She sat up as it opened, relieved to find she was fully dressed even if it meant she had nothing clean to wear.

'Good morning, you two sleepyheads.'

Regan grimaced. 'Sorry.'

'Don't apologise. You obviously needed the sleep,' Chase said as he skirted the bed and reached out to Phoebe, who scrambled into his arms.

The sight of him cuddling his daughter did something strange to Regan's stomach. Or maybe she needed breakfast. She heard laughter from the open door. 'Are the boys up already?'

'Yes. Up, showered and breakfasted.'

'Oh, my God. I'm so sorry.' While Phoebe slid down Chase's body to the floor, Regan swung her legs over the side of the bed. When she looked up again, he met her eyes and smiled a tender, understanding smile which took her breath away.

'Don't worry. We managed without a plan.'

'I'm not worried. I'm embarrassed.'

'Well, don't be. Come and have some breakfast.'

A little while later in the other room, Chase insisted on Regan and Phoebe sitting at the heavy pine table while he served them cereal and toast.

'Mummy,' Cory said, standing beside her chair, 'Chase said we can swim with sea lions today if you say we can. *Please*, Mum, say we can.'

She glanced over his head at Chase, who had the grace

to look sheepish. He came to stand behind Cory but, before he could speak, Will piped up.

'Do we have to go home? Do you have to go to work, Mum?'

She felt her heart twist in her chest at the plea in his voice. Her boys wanted to swim with sea lions. What sort of mother would she be if she packed them up and took them home? Surely they didn't think she'd make them leave?

She loved these boys. She wanted them to be happy. She would like to believe she always put their needs first.

Chase was watching her face. He stepped around Cory and touched her shoulder lightly.

'I'm sorry, it's my fault. I shouldn't have mentioned it before checking with you.'

'No, it's fine.' She looked up at Chase. 'But is it safe?'

'Absolutely. We do it all the time.' He tipped his head towards Phoebe. 'Don't we, Sweetpea?'

'I like the sea lions,' Phoebe said. 'And they like me.'

Regan nodded. 'I'm sure they do. I'm sure they'll like Will and Cory, too.'

Will's face lit up. 'We can stay?'

'Mum? Can we?' Cory asked in an awed whisper.

She nodded. 'I'll have to make a couple of phone calls to check everything's all right at work, but yes, we can stay.'

Cory hugged her. 'When can we go? Can we go now?'

'Not yet, Cory,' Chase interrupted. 'Let your mum eat her breakfast in peace. She'll want to shower, too. Don't forget she's only just woken up.'

Cory nodded and went to sit on the sofa but Chase stopped him. 'We could go and kick the footy for a while?'

'Yes!'

Regan's chest tightened. This was what her sons had missed out on.

Chase grinned at her. 'I think I said the right thing.'

'You certainly did.'

'Can I leave you to help Phoebe get dressed? I'll get her clothes out before I go.'

'Sure.' She smiled at Phoebe. 'Is that all right with you, sweetie?'

'Uh-huh,' Phoebe said, nodding.

Chase disappeared for a minute, reappearing with a ball under his arm. 'Okay, guys. Let's go.' He dropped a kiss on the top of Phoebe's head, then, as he passed, brushed Regan's cheek with his fingertips.

It was the lightest, most innocent touch, but it sent a tremor through her insides and made her thoughts scoot all over the place.

How could he do this to her with just a touch?

She'd have to be very careful if she was going to avoid falling for him. And she had to avoid it because, if she didn't, she'd risk having her heart broken again. She knew better than to want to repeat that devastating experience.

And she would not let her sons be rejected for a second time. By *any* man.

CHAPTER SIX

REGAN called after Chase as he headed out with her sons, 'Do we need to bring anything for the swim?'

He turned at the door. 'Nothing. Just yourselves. Sunscreen is banned before the swim but you can bring some to put on in the boat afterwards. Wetsuits and snorkels are provided.'

'Wetsuits?' That was just great. What would she look like in a wetsuit? A stick insect. And she thought he'd already seen her at her worst. She shook her head. 'You know, I think I'll sit it out. I'll come with you, but I won't go in the water.'

Chase frowned and came back into the room. 'Why not? You can swim, can't you?'

'Yes, I can swim.'

'Regan...' Chase pushed a hand through his hair. 'I don't want you to miss out on the experience. You'll enjoy it, I promise.'

'Don't worry about me.'

His expression surprisingly serious, he said, 'I can't help it.'

She opened her mouth to scoff but suddenly the thought

of a man—this particular man—worrying about her filled her throat with emotion and robbed her of the power of speech.

'Please, Regan. Come into the water with us.' He came to squat beside her chair. 'You'll enjoy sharing the experience with the boys. Trust me.'

He was so close. She had an urge to reach out and stroke his face, to feel how smooth his jaw was so soon after shaving. But, with an effort, she held back. After a convulsive swallow, she found her voice—not that it sounded like hers.

'Okay.' It didn't matter what she looked like. It didn't matter what he thought of her. If she kept repeating the words to herself, she just might start to believe them.

Regan dropped the hand she'd been using to shade her eyes when Jan came to sit next to her on the bench seat at the side of the boat.

'Makes a nice picture, doesn't it?'

Regan glanced at Chase with the three children gathered around him as he pointed out items of interest from the other side of the *Explorer*. She'd been thinking the same thing but she wasn't about to admit it. 'The boys love facts and figures, especially Will. You don't have any children, Jan?'

She saw a flash of pain in Jan's eyes before she smiled. 'I never managed to have children of my own. I've accepted that it's too late now. The sea lions are like my kids. And then there's Phoebe, of course. I feel so sorry for her, having to grow up without a mother.'

'Yes, but lots of children have single parents and they grow up okay. I'm a single parent, Jan.'

'I know.' Jan frowned. 'But you work and your sons go to school. It's not the same. I don't think it's good for either of them the way Chase has cut himself off from other people.

He says it keeps things simple.' She glanced at Regan's face. 'You know you're the first woman he's dated?'

'We're not dating,' she said quickly. 'We're just friends.'

Jan smiled. 'My mistake.'

'Are we nearly there?' Regan asked, changing the subject smoothly.

'Yep. Then you'll transfer into the flat-bottomed boat.' She jerked her head at the small boat being towed behind the motor launch. 'Because the spot where we do the swims is a shallow pool.'

'The bay's much bigger than I thought, bigger than it looks.'

'That's because it's actually an inlet. There are several small bays around the shore.'

Regan nibbled on her bottom lip. 'What about sharks?'

'There are Great Whites out in the Bight but they don't come in here because the mouth of the inlet is too shallow. Don't worry, the boys will be safe.'

Regan smiled her thanks for the reassurance.

'Hey, kids,' Jan called across the boat. 'After lunch, you can help me catch some fish for tea.'

'We don't know how to fish,' Will said, his face serious.

Phoebe jumped up and down. 'I do.'

'We'll show you,' Jan said. 'We've got loads of spare rods and tackle. And you two can have the afternoon to yourselves,' she said, smiling from Regan to Chase.

'Unless Regan has to get home,' Chase said.

Will exchanged an excited glance with Cory and, seeing their faces, Regan knew she couldn't spoil their fun. It wouldn't hurt to stay a few hours longer and, having made her phone calls earlier, she was confident she wouldn't be needed.

'No, that's fine,' she said with a smile for all of them.
Mike cut the boat engine and within moments Jan had organized adults and children alike into the smaller boat.

'Aren't you coming?' Regan called when she saw Jan had stayed aboard the *Explorer*.

'No, someone needs to stay here,' she shouted back. 'Mike will look after you. Have a great time.'

Regan put her arm around Cory's shoulders as he bounced on the aluminium seat beside her. 'Exciting, isn't it?'

Cory grinned up at her and love swelled her heart. She wished she could make every weekend so much fun for her sons. After her own upbringing, she was only too aware of the importance of a happy childhood—and she'd thought she was doing a good job of ensuring her boys had one. She knew she'd done the best she could, but she'd do even better if she could find more time. Now that the Japanese restaurant contract was settled...

But that was something to think about later. For now, she grinned back at Cory and, with her grin still in place, glanced over her shoulder. She caught Chase's eye and he gave her a look of such approval that when she faced the front again she felt a glow like warm honey trickling through her veins.

'Look!' Will cried.

Following his pointing finger, Regan saw her first sea lion, swimming alongside and at the same speed as the boat. As she watched, it left the water in a small leap. She squeezed Cory as the creature leapt again.

From the tiller at the back of the boat, Mike's gruff voice reached them. 'He's telling you he wants someone to play with.'

'There's another one,' Cory yelled. 'And another.'

The boat came to a standstill and preparations took a few minutes as Mike handed out masks and snorkels, helping the boys to put them on and demonstrating how to use them.

Regan glanced at Chase, who was assisting Phoebe. He looked up. 'Need any help?'

'No. I haven't used one of these for years but I still remember how.'

Moments later, they were all ready. Chase slipped quietly into the water and reached up to help the children, one by one. Regan joined them, sliding into the cool water without a splash. As she swam towards the boys, a sea lion broke the surface right next to her. He dived beneath her and came up on the other side. Surprised, she trod water, watching him, and chuckled when he flipped into an identical vertical position.

She could swear he was mimicking her.

After a moment, he tipped his head to one side and she copied him. Then he tipped it to the other side and she did the same.

She heard the children laugh. This was weird. She was playing games with a wild creature.

Suddenly, he swam around her and dived, surfaced and dived again. Chase had joined her and he called to the boys to follow the sea lion underwater.

'Did you see that?' she asked him.

He nodded. 'Come on. Let's go and play.'

Underwater, Regan saw that Jan had been right about the pool being shallow. She could stand on her hands on the sandy ocean bottom and wave her feet above water if she wanted to. And it was as clear as bottled water. With no major industrial facilities within a hundred miles or more, the west coast of the Eyre Peninsula was totally pollution-free.

She watched a sea lion swim right up to Will and touch his mask with its nose, its huge brown eyes inquisitive, while another swam circles around Cory, urging him to join in his game.

Within seconds a sea lion had swum between her legs and she followed it, touching the ocean floor between patches of seagrass, then pushing back up to the surface.

Twisting and diving, the creature led her below again. It was bizarre but she had no doubt it wanted her to play. She kept a watchful eye on the boys at first, but soon began to relax. They were clearly having a great time and Chase was there.

By the time they returned to the small boat where Mike awaited them, Regan was enthralled by the intelligence and gentle nature of the playful mammals.

When she and Chase had helped the children into the boat and were the only ones left in the water, she removed her mask and snorkel. He took them from her and tossed them up to Mike along with his own.

'Enjoy that?' he asked.

'Oh, boy, do you need to ask? I've never, *never* done anything that was so much fun. It was amazing. They seem to enjoy it, too, don't they?'

'The sea lions? No doubt about it. They wouldn't do it otherwise. They've never been fed or enticed in any way. They want to play with people.'

She was a little breathless after all the activity and excitement and her words came out in a rush. 'You are *so* lucky to be able to do that any time you want. I envy you.'

He looked thoughtful but, before he could say anything, Mike called out, 'Come on, guys, let's get back to the *Explorer* for some tucker.'

* * *

Back on board, they found that Jan had prepared lunch and the children tucked into sandwiches while Mike turned the boat around and headed back to shore.

Chase sat next to Regan and held out a plate of sandwiches to her. He watched her take a sandwich and bite into it, the excited sparkle still in her eyes. He enjoyed seeing her like this. 'I'm glad you decided to come with us.'

She swallowed before she looked into his eyes. 'Not half as glad as I am,' she said with feeling. 'I can't believe I nearly missed that. I've heard people enthuse about swimming with dolphins. I suppose it's very similar.'

'It is, but it's also different.'

'You've done it?'

'Mike and Jan take people out to swim with dolphins, too. They're further out, in deeper water. Again, they've never been fed so they don't come for food like the dolphins in some other places.'

'How is it different?'

'The best explanation I can come up with is that dolphins are like cats and sea lions are like dogs. Dolphins are aloof. They tolerate humans and allow them to interact but only when they feel like it. It's a privilege to swim with them and there's a magical quality about it.

'Sea lions, on the other hand, love people and just want to play.'

She smiled. 'That explains it perfectly.' She ate in silence for a moment, then said, 'The boys keep asking me for a dog.'

'You don't want to get one?'

She hesitated. 'I don't have the time to look after one and I don't think I could ask Mum to do it.'

He felt a twinge of disappointment on behalf of the

boys. He knew they'd enjoy growing up with a dog—as he would have done himself if he'd had the chance. He'd craved the devotion a dog would have shown him. He'd needed to feel someone—even if that someone was only a dog—cared about him above all others.

He tilted his head as a thought occurred to him. Perhaps he should get one for Phoebe. It might help to make up for the isolation that Jan kept pointing out. He'd like to think she didn't feel unloved. He'd committed his life to ensuring that she didn't. But she could still benefit from the company.

He offered the plate to Regan and was surprised when she took another sandwich. 'We'll fatten you up yet,' he said without thinking.

Her eyes widened. 'It must be the exercise. You think I'm too thin?'

He made a rocking motion with one hand. 'On the thin side.'

Her face fell and she looked away.

He winced; he hadn't meant to upset her. 'Not that you aren't beautiful.'

Her head snapped back. 'You think I'm beautiful?' Her voice was incredulous.

He took a deep breath. He hadn't meant to get personal. He wasn't sure exactly where the boundary lay between friendship and more-than-friends when it came to conversations like this.

'I think you're very beautiful. Now, what would you like to do this afternoon?'

'I have no idea.' She gave him a rueful smile. 'Of course, I had intended to go into the office.'

'Would you like to go for a drive?'

'Where to?'

She began to scrape her wet hair off her face as she spoke and he wanted to reach out and help, but he kept his hands to himself.

Where to?

He wanted to share his favourite place with Regan. Surely friends would share such things? It didn't have to mean he was trying to pull her further into his life.

It was the place he always visited when he needed peace and solitude. Maybe he suspected she too needed the peace it brought. It had always worked for him.

'I'd like to show you a spot that not many people know about. It's quiet and peaceful and very special to me. But I'll understand if you'd rather stay near the boys.'

He watched her blue eyes widen. They were an exact match for the sky behind her and, as he stared into them for an endless moment, he felt as if the movement of the boat was pitching him forward. What she said then would have kicked his feet out from under him if he hadn't been sitting.

'I'd be honoured.'

Her voice was a soft whisper, not like her normal voice at all, and made him think of the way she'd felt in his arms when he'd carried her to bed. He didn't want to think about *why* that image had come to mind. He tried to block it. He had to back off before he did or said something he'd regret.

'Okay, that's what we'll do then,' he said briskly as he got to his feet. 'I need to have a word with Mike. I'll catch up with you later.'

Sitting in the passenger seat of Chase's four-wheel drive vehicle, Regan puzzled over her reaction to his suggestion. Why had she been so moved by the thought of seeing a place that was special to him? The fact that he'd chosen to take her there didn't mean he saw her as special, too. But she'd felt an incredible connection to him once he'd suggested it and the look in his eyes had sent a tremor through her. She'd almost forgotten how to breathe.

That all seemed very silly now. He'd shown no sign of having been affected by the moment. Its deeper significance must have existed only in her imagination—the result of heightened emotions after her extraordinary swim.

He caught her watching him and flashed a smile. 'We have to park just up here and walk the rest of the way. I hope that's okay?'

'And if I say no?'

His smile slipped. 'Is walking a problem?'

'No, of course not. I was only teasing.' She took off her seat belt as he brought the vehicle to a standstill. 'Is it far?'

'A bit of a walk. Not too far.'

He reached into the rear footwell for a backpack while she opened the door and slid down to the ground. She stood for a moment, breathing deeply and gazing at the wide expanse of unspoilt sand dunes and native vegetation.

As he strode around the car, pulling the straps of the backpack on to his shoulders, he smiled. 'Can you hear that?' He tilted his head to the side.

'What?'

'Shh. Listen.'

She tore her eyes away from his broad, square shoulders which the straps emphasised, from the muscles evident through his white T-shirt, and listened. After a long moment, she frowned up at him. 'I can't hear a thing.'

'Exactly. Total silence.'

She nodded, understanding.

'This way. The track's narrow, I'm afraid.'

He was right. She couldn't walk at his side so she

followed him for several minutes, trying to keep her eyes on the track at her feet and not on his tall, athletic physique. In spite of her determination, her gaze roamed to his tanned, muscular calves, and then upwards.

Chase came to an abrupt halt at a place where the track opened out and dropped down sharply towards the beach. He reached for her hand but his eyes were fixed on something ahead of him. She slipped her hand into his, noting that it looked starkly pale in comparison, and let him pull her close to his side.

'Look,' he said, pointing at a large bird patrolling the sky near the edge of the water.

She watched as it stopped its hypnotic, back-and-forth flight and hovered. Suddenly it plunged feet first into the water, disappearing beneath the surface. She held her breath, then gasped as the bird burst from the ocean with a fish in its talons. Making a *chip-chip* sound, it flew towards the sand dunes on their left, where it vanished from sight.

'Wow,' she said. 'What was that?'

'An osprey.'

'Really? I've never seen one before.'

'They're rare in southern Australia and they're becoming even more rare because of coastal development.' He shook his head. 'Their habitat is being destroyed so that people can build houses in places like this.' He swung his free hand towards the dunes.

'You'd think we'd have learned from our mistakes in the past, but no. Now we're in danger of repeating those environmental blunders for the sake of coastal development. I don't mean a few shacks built behind the dunes like Leo Bay, I mean—'

He stopped.

Regan could see real concern etched on his face before he wiped it off and gave her a half smile. Her stomach twitched. 'Go on,' she said, moistening her lips.

'No. I didn't bring you here to listen to me ranting. I want to show you something. Come on.'

It seemed natural for him to keep hold of her hand as he headed into the dunes and she knew he'd slowed his pace to suit her. She'd already begun to breathe quite heavily and didn't think she could walk much further in comfort.

After a short time, Chase came to a stop and pointed to a bush in front of him. An ordinary-looking bush.

Regan sucked in a deep breath. 'What's so interesting about this?' she asked, flapping her hand at the bush.

A pair of delicate blue butterflies took flight, danced in front of her eyes and fluttered away.

'Oh.' She sighed. 'Did I frighten them off?'

Chase nodded. 'But you weren't to know. I only knew they were there because I saw them land. Pretty aren't they?'

'Yes.' She sighed again as they disappeared from sight. 'Are they rare too?'

'In some areas. You see, they're dependent on that species of shrub,' he said, pointing at the same bush, 'and it only grows behind sand dunes. When the dunes are cleared to make way for development, the butterflies are wiped out, too.'

'What a shame.' She pulled a hand across her damp forehead. 'I need to sit for a minute.'

He swung round and took a good look at her as she flopped to the ground. 'Don't you feel well?' Sliding the backpack off his shoulders, he dug inside it and brought out a bottle of water wrapped in an ice pack. 'Here, have a drink.'

He dropped down beside her and opened the bottle before handing it to her.

She took it gratefully. 'I'm fine. Just not used to walking, especially on a hot day. I'd normally be in the office now, remember.'

After gulping several mouthfuls of water and taking some deep breaths, she gave him a curious look. 'Have you got into all this environmental stuff since you've lived in Leo Bay? It doesn't seem to sit with the image of a corporate lawyer.'

'I didn't give any of it a second thought when I lived in the city. I'm a different person now.'

She hesitated, then decided she felt comfortable enough with him to say what was on her mind. 'There are lawyers who specialise in environmental cases, aren't there? You could move into that field, couldn't you?'

He turned to face her. 'Yes, there are. I can't say I've thought about it. I've always assumed that if I went back to work, I'd go back to my own specialisation, to what I know.'

'But you know the environment now. At least, you know what needs to be done to protect it. You'd learn anything else you needed to know.' She tilted her head and gave him a questioning look. 'And who says you have to go back full-time? You could work part-time when Phoebe starts school. Even before then.'

He took her hand and ran his thumb over the back of it, setting off a chain reaction in her skin that rippled right through her.

'Are you ashamed of your friend, the beach bum?'

She sucked in a sharp breath. 'It's not that. It's just... you said you missed the challenge of work. And the environment is something you care about. I thought it would be something you'd enjoy.' She turned her head away and stared at the ground. 'I'm sorry if you don't like the idea.'

After a moment of silence he said, 'I do.'

He cupped her cheek with his free hand and gently forced her to look at him again. With an effort, she resisted rubbing her cheek against his palm. Just.

'I like the idea, but I really like that you care enough to suggest it.'

'You mean, you're going to do it?'

'I'm going to think about it. I won't rush into anything. I don't want to do something that will disrupt Phoebe's life. I don't want to do anything that might get complicated.'

For a moment, she stared. Was he still talking about work? Or did he mean her…them?

He caressed her cheek, smoothing his thumb lightly across the skin. A soft gasp escaped from her throat when he bent his head and kissed her other cheek.

Slowly, he lowered his gaze to her lips and his warm brown eyes became intent.

Her body reacted as if it had a mind of its own, every nerve screaming with anticipation, the only sound her heartbeat thudding in her ears. This acute physical response to him was something new to her. She'd never known anything like it. She wanted…no, she was desperate to feel his lips on hers.

And, when she felt them, she shivered.

The kiss was brief. His lips pressed gently against hers for an instant. Barely long enough for her to register the firmness of his mouth, the heat of it against her water-cooled lips. But long enough to stop her heart. Long enough to fill the empty spaces inside her with an expectant, aching need.

He pulled back and stared at her, his eyes wide. She had a moment of confused hope before reality came crashing in.

Kissing him was a bad idea.

A very bad idea.

What had she been thinking? She'd had every intention of guarding her heart, and here she was…doing anything but.

An anguished moan broke from her and Chase dropped his hand as if she'd burned him.

'What? Regan, what's wrong?'

She shook her head. 'We're supposed to be friends.'

'We are.'

She shook her head again. 'I'm not looking for… anything else. I certainly don't want a romantic relationship.'

He got to his feet and rubbed the back of his neck. 'Nor me. Believe me, I didn't intend…'

She stared up at his troubled face. No. She knew it to be the truth. He wasn't over his wife's death. He'd made it clear he didn't want anything to disrupt his straightfor-ward life with his daughter. And a romance would defi-nitely do that.

She felt she knew him well enough to be sure that a casual fling wasn't on his agenda, either.

So what had just happened between them?

She'd been attracted to him since they'd met, she realised now. She'd been bewildered by the feeling. She hadn't believed it. Hadn't accepted it. But it had been there all along.

Now, it seemed that Chase might have been fighting the same feelings.

It wasn't his fault, what had happened. She'd been wrong to put herself in this position.

Chase dropped to a crouch in front of her. 'Listen, it doesn't have to change anything. We can pretend it never happened. Can't we?' She saw his Adam's apple bob while he waited for her answer.

'I guess.' She wasn't so sure, but she knew it was what he wanted to hear. She took another drink of cool water from the bottle, then handed it back to him. 'What did you bring me down here to show me?'

He frowned. 'What?'

'You wanted to show me something.'

After searching her face for a moment longer, he nodded. He stood and held out a hand to pull her up. 'How are you feeling now? Are you up to walking further?'

'I'm fine.' She cleared her throat before taking his hand, making a conscious effort to ignore the effect of the contact. 'It's not too far now, is it?'

'No. Just a little way.'

As she brushed sand from her skirt, she slid a surreptitious glance at him. Her stomach lurched at the worry and guilt in his face. She wanted to hug him and tell him it wasn't his fault, that she'd been just as much to blame. That she'd wanted the kiss every bit as much as he had. Maybe more.

But that would be a bad move.

For a second there was raw pain in his eyes and she knew it was Larissa he was thinking about. There was nothing she could say or do that would ease his burden.

He looked up and his expression softened when their eyes met. 'Ready?'

She nodded.

When Chase stopped walking, he pointed ahead. 'See those?'

'What? Those piles of sticks?'

'Yes.' He smiled. 'They're osprey nests. Great, aren't they?'

'Amazing. They're huge.'

He nodded. 'That's what makes this place special for me. Sometimes, when Phoebe's with Jan, I just sit here and watch the parent birds coming and going. I don't think they could fail to notice me but they obviously don't consider me a threat.'

As she watched him, she worked hard to swallow a lump of regret. He was gorgeous to look at—and she hadn't thought that way about a man since Jack—but it was more than his looks that made her ache. He had more depth and more kindness in his little finger than Jack had ever possessed.

She'd wanted him to kiss her and that knowledge scared her to death because, fantastic as he was, he was still a man. He might not be a threat to the osprey and their young, but he could become a threat to her and her sons.

Because all three of them were vulnerable to a man like Chase. They'd all been rejected by Jack. They all had empty spaces in their hearts that Chase could fill. And instinct told her that he would, if she wasn't careful. She was too honest to deny that it would be all too easy to fall into a relationship with him.

But Chase had already given his heart away. To his wife. And it was clear that he still considered it hers. She couldn't risk getting involved with him only to find that he wasn't ready for another woman.

It would mean hurt and rejection. It might not come in the near future, but it would come. And her boys did not deserve to be rejected again. She had to keep them safe.

And the only way she could think of was to leave and not come back. To remove all of them, but especially herself, from a situation that threatened their emotional security.

With his hands resting on his hips, Chase was half-turned away from her but, from what she could see of his face, he no longer appeared to be looking at the nests. He was lost in thought.

'Chase?' she said softly.

'Hmm?'

'I'd like to go back now.'

'Right.' He jerked into movement and turned to head back the way they'd come.

'And I think the boys and I had better go home—as soon as they've finished fishing,' she said as she fell in beside him.

His footsteps didn't falter. Without looking at her, he said, 'Sure. I understand.'

Regan's chest seemed to cram into her throat. He hadn't made the slightest attempt to talk her out of leaving. And that hurt.

It shouldn't. She was being illogical. The very idea that she wanted him to try to talk her out of it made her a total idiot. But she knew that if she'd suggested leaving half an hour ago, he'd have come up with a good reason why she and the boys should hang around longer.

Now, he didn't want them to stay and she pined for what they'd had before everything had changed. He'd suggested they could forget about the kiss, pretend it had never happened, but they couldn't. As brief as it had been, it was a symbol of something much bigger. Of their inability to be friends without their attraction getting in the way. It seemed that Chase had realised the truth and was as keen as her to be out of the difficult situation they'd found themselves in.

The drive back to his house passed in near silence. Regan stared out of the window and fought to restrain the tears that burned at the back of her eyes. She tried to think about anything but the fact that she was about to leave and would never see Chase again.

Because she wouldn't. She was sure of it.

This had been their opportunity to see if they could establish a platonic friendship that would last and they'd blown it.

It had been a short friendship, but it had been amazing. She'd never forget this weekend, the things they'd done, but especially the way she'd felt. She'd never forget how safe she'd felt with him, even though she knew that security was just an illusion.

CHAPTER SEVEN

As REGAN drove towards Port Lincoln, her thoughts wouldn't leave Leo Bay. The disappointment on the boys' faces had been hard to take when they'd been told the visit had come to an end. Combined with her own reluctance to leave Chase, Phoebe and their lovely, relaxed home, Regan felt as if her heart were being put through a mincer. But she had to stay strong. Later—much later—she'd look back on this time and know she'd done the right thing.

Wouldn't she?

The regret would fade and she'd be left feeling relieved that she'd been proactive. That she'd taken action to ensure a secure future for all of them.

Besides, Chase had withdrawn into himself. He was still friendly and generous towards Will and Cory and, hopefully, they'd noticed nothing, but she'd detected a difference. A distance which signified to her that he was in the same frame of mind as herself.

She knew he didn't dislike her personally, so it must be the idea of being disloyal to Larissa that had him feeling guilt or grief or any one of the myriad emotions a widower must feel in these circumstances.

He'd packed in ice the fish they'd caught and cleaned

with Jan, helped them to gather the toys and books they'd brought, hosed down and dried the two bodyboards and loaded them into the car, and wrapped up the remaining birthday cake for them. All with a smile but with a wariness in his eyes that hadn't been there before.

As they'd got into the car, Will had asked when—not if—they could come again, and Chase had ruffled his hair and mumbled something vague about them being welcome any time. It had satisfied Will but it had torn at her insides.

She'd climbed into the car without a word, ashamed at her bad manners but unable to trust herself to speak. She hadn't even been able to thank him for the wonderful time they'd had. She'd had to get away as quickly as possible. And once she'd got the car started, she hadn't looked back.

Chase watched Regan drive away and then stood at the side of the road, staring at nothing. This was the second time he'd watched her leave. The first occasion had stung but hadn't been anywhere near as painful as this time.

She'd been right to leave. He knew that. But now that he'd spent hours in her company, he also knew it was going to be damned difficult to dig her out from under his skin. It was right to get a barbed fish hook out of a finger, but that didn't make the removal any less painful.

He grimaced at the comparison. She'd hooked him, despite his determination not to betray Larissa's memory. She'd hooked him without trying, without even wanting to.

The more he'd seen of her, the more he'd liked her.

That was the thing—he *liked* Regan. *And* desired her, he admitted now.

It was the desire that had made him want to kiss her. Her cheek had felt so smooth beneath his palm. Her hair had smelt of apples. Her lips had looked so inviting. It had seemed so right.

But afterwards her expressive blue eyes had shown shock, confusion and dismay. Not the emotions a man wanted a woman to feel right after he kissed her. Yet he understood them. He'd felt confused himself. Confused, angry and disappointed.

Angry because Larissa deserved better from him. She deserved to be remembered, not to have her memory obliterated by a rush of hormones. And it had been a hell of a rush, shocking him with the effort it took to pull away from Regan, to keep the kiss brief.

Disappointed because he'd known that he'd ruined his friendship with Regan. Earlier in the day, he'd worried about overstepping the boundaries of their friendship with his words. This afternoon he'd stomped all over those boundaries without a second thought.

Regan had made it very clear that she wanted nothing more than friendship and he understood where she was coming from. After the damage her ex-husband had done, she was entitled to be distrustful where men were concerned.

If she was his, he'd never leave her.

Now where had that thought come from? Dismissing it, he reminded himself that he didn't want a relationship, either. In fact, he'd thought he'd found the perfect solution to his loneliness—because he had been lonely, he realised now. He'd found someone he enjoyed being around, someone he liked, who was great with his daughter, and who didn't want anything from him but his company.

It had been perfect. But he'd messed it up.

He didn't need anything complicated and he knew instinctively that a relationship with Regan would be full on.

But it would be worth the effort.

And where had *that* thought come from? He threw up his hands in frustration. He couldn't even control his own thoughts. What hope did he have with his hormones?

'Why are you standing here, Daddy?'

He started. He hadn't noticed Phoebe tugging on the leg of his jeans. He'd better pull himself together.

'Hey, Sweetpea. Want something to eat?'

She shook her head. 'When are Will and Cory coming back?'

He coughed away the sudden obstruction in his throat. 'I don't know.'

'I didn't want them to go.'

He glanced around, looking for something to distract his daughter from a subject he didn't want to discuss, but when he caught sight of Jan heading towards them, he groaned.

'What's wrong, Daddy? Do you have a tummy ache?'

'Yes,' he said. 'Something like that.'

Jan held up two small fishing rods. 'I brought these for the boys. They might as well keep them here.'

Chase shook his head, his throat aching now.

Jan gave him a blank look. 'Why not?'

'Phoebe, will you pop inside and make sure I didn't leave the television on?'

She looked surprised but skipped across the gravel driveway to the front steps.

'They've gone home, Jan. They won't be back.'

'What? Never?'

'Never.'

Disbelief filled her face for a moment, then she glanced at the space Regan's car had occupied. 'Well, that's a damn shame. I liked them.'

He pressed his lips together.

'And it was really good to see you so happy.'

'I'm happy as I am, Jan.'

She waved away his words and glanced towards the house. 'I know you loved Larissa,' she said in a low voice, 'but she's gone, Chase. And you and Regan would have been good together.'

'How could you possibly know that?'

'Because I'm not blind?'

He grunted.

'The kids got on really well.'

'Yes.' He shoved his hands in his pockets. 'I know.'

'So …?'

He shook his head. 'I'm going in,' he said abruptly and turned to the steps.

'I'll take the fishing rods home, then?'

'Yes, you'd better do that,' he said in a gentler tone.

He closed the door and leaned against it.

He'd wanted to show Regan some fun. The boys, too. He'd wanted to make their lives that little bit brighter than they'd been when they'd met. He'd done that, he was sure, but for such a short time. The last thing he'd wanted to do was hurt her. He liked her too much.

She was such a caring person. He'd been moved by the knowledge that she'd been thinking about his situation. Her suggestion was a good one. He might look into the possibility of using his legal expertise for the benefit of the environment. But it wasn't the idea as much as the thought behind it that moved him. He couldn't remember anyone caring about what he needed before.

His parents certainly hadn't cared, and Larissa… well, it would have shocked him if she'd taken his needs into consideration. She never had, he admitted now. Right to the end.

His chest filled with the familiar pain of his wife's life-or-death decision. But this time his thoughts didn't linger on Larissa. Because he was thinking about Regan and, yes, it was desire that had led him to kiss her, but it was *liking* her that would make him miss her like mad.

By the time the boys had eaten and were ready for bed, Regan was exhausted both physically and mentally and couldn't help being glad when they said they were too tired for a story. She normally loved their bedtime ritual. She adored the good-natured squabble over which bed she should sit on while she read to them, even though she was always careful to alternate between the two. And she cherished the moment she took after they'd fallen asleep to sit quietly and appreciate what she had.

Tonight, though, for once, she couldn't wait to be alone as she made her way to the bedroom the boys shared.

The house looked as if they'd never been away. Or rather, she thought, grimacing, as if they'd never lived there. Not like Chase's house. Now *that* was a proper home.

This house was a model of organisation. Tidiness saved time, she'd always said, and the boys had learned the lesson well. Even in their own room. She'd always been grateful for that but now she wondered, what was she raising—boys or robots?

Time wasn't as tight now that the business was doing well. She could afford to lighten up. And she would. She'd make a point of looking for ways to make her schedule less demanding.

Being with Chase had made her feel that somewhere

along the way—somewhere between running the business and making sure the boys had everything they should have—she'd forgotten about herself. She'd confined her emotional needs to those that involved being a mother. But she was also a woman and she deserved to take some time out to do the things that women did. Some of her single friends swore by day spas and luxurious beauty treatments. She wasn't sure that sort of thing was really for her, but she would give it some thought. It wasn't exactly on a par with kissing Chase, but that particular type of relaxation was out of the question.

Whatever she came up with, it went without saying that she wouldn't let it keep her from her children. She wouldn't turn into a clone of her father.

Her father was the one she'd idolised, the parent she'd wanted to spend time with. He was the one whose lap she'd wanted to crawl on to, whose stories she'd wanted to hear. But the occasions when he'd had time for her had been so few and far between that she could probably count them on one hand if she put her mind to it.

She hadn't been the dainty little doll he'd wanted in a daughter. She'd always been tall for her age and gawky with it. Her legs and arms had seemed too long for her body and, combined with an innate lack of coordination they'd made her look and feel clumsy.

With her friends she hadn't felt out of place even though she'd stood head and shoulders taller than most of them. But, at home, she'd been a klutz. She hadn't done anything right and her father's impatience with her had hurt.

She didn't want to think about that, though. She didn't want to dredge up the hurt she'd felt when, time after time, he'd turned her away from his study saying he had to work and he'd see her later. Only later had never come. She'd struggled to stay awake at night so she'd know if he came into her room. But he rarely did. She'd sometimes receive messages from him via her mother and she'd fizz inside at the knowledge that he'd thought of her. But, most of the time, he was too busy to remember.

They hadn't taken family holidays. He hadn't gone to her school events. She'd had material things—toys, books, clothes. He'd been a good provider, but she hadn't had *him*. Not really.

She'd never wanted her boys to have similar childhood memories and, when Jack had left, she'd been determined to ensure they never felt neglected, even if they only had one parent to care about them.

From habit, she tucked in Cory first and he gave her a weary smile.

'I had the *best* time, Mum.'

She kissed him. 'I'm glad, darling. Goodnight. Sleep tight.'

Tears sprang to her eyes but she brushed them away with the back of her hand before turning to Will. She would let them fall later. When she was alone.

Will kept his face to the wall when she moved to his bedside.

'Will?'

Sighing, he rolled his head towards her. 'Mum, did Dad leave because he didn't like us? Me and Cory?'

'What? *No.* No, of course not.' She wound her arms around his shoulders. She couldn't hold the tears back any longer and they trickled into Will's hair. 'You mustn't think that way, Will. Daddy left for all sorts of reasons, but not because of you. Definitely not.'

Her voice thick with tears, she forced herself to speak firmly. 'He loves you,' she said as convincingly as she could.

She'd seen no evidence of her claim in recent years, but Jack had been happy at Will's birth. And at Cory's. They'd both been happy.

'But does he *like* us?'

She hesitated, her mind working frantically to come up with an answer that would satisfy him. If Will understood the difference between liking and loving, he was more perceptive than she'd given him credit for.

With a sigh, she said, 'Look, Will, your father had problems of his own which had nothing to do with whether he liked you or not. Please don't blame yourself. It wasn't your fault.'

Will regarded her silently for a long moment. 'I think Chase likes us.'

Cory sat up. 'I like Chase, too.'

Regan rubbed her forehead. She'd hardly noticed her headache while she'd been at Leo Bay but now she was home it had returned even worse than before.

'Naturally you like him,' she said. 'He's a nice man.' She took a deep breath. 'And of course he likes both of you. I mean, what is there not to like?'

Cory giggled and flopped down again.

Will rolled on to his side. 'So when can we go to Leo Bay again?'

She opened her mouth but closed it when she couldn't think what to say. She didn't want to give him false hope, but she couldn't bring herself to refuse him, either. Not at this moment. There was too much emotion in the air.

'We'll see,' she said.

'Does that mean next weekend?'

'That means we'll talk about it some other time but not now because it's time to go to sleep.'

Will yawned. His eyes closed and Regan heaved a silent sigh, grateful that he wasn't about to press her for an answer.

After a quick shower, she went to bed herself, desperate for sleep but unable to drop off. She couldn't stop thinking about what—and who—she'd left behind today. How long would this last? she wondered. How long before she'd be able to get a decent night's sleep? She'd only just met the man. By rights, she should get over him in a flash. But somehow she didn't think logic stood a chance. Instinct told her it would be a long time before she forgot Chase, before she stopped wondering what he was doing and what it would have felt like if they'd gone on with the kiss.

She closed her eyes and touched her cheek, remembering the sweep of his thumb as he'd held her face. It would have been so easy to lean into him, to demand more from the kiss.

But instead she'd chosen short-term pain over long-term suffering. Tearing herself away had been the equivalent of ripping off a dressing. Trouble was, it had left behind a gaping wound. And it hurt.

Just as Regan and the boys were finishing a lazy Sunday breakfast, her mother turned up.

'How's Pop?' Regan asked, pouring tea into an extra cup.

'He's okay. Well, actually, he's…a little confused.'

Regan handed over the cup of tea with a questioning look.

'He needs someone to look after him.'

'Oh.' She considered for a moment. 'We have space here. Spare rooms. I'd love him to move in. The boys would like it, too.'

Her mother sighed. 'No. I suggested it already but he

won't have a bar of it. He won't leave the house where he lived all his married life.'

Regan frowned. 'That makes it difficult.'

'The only solution is for me to move in with him and take care of him.'

'Oh.' Regan settled back in her chair with her cup. 'Yes, that's probably the best option. But are you sure it won't be too much for you, Mum?'

'It won't be too much, but I know this is going to be hard for you with the boys. You do understand, don't you, Regan? I want to look after my father while he's still here. I don't know how much longer he'll be around for.'

'Of course I understand, Mum—who wouldn't? And don't worry about me or the boys; we'll manage somehow. What's important is you spend time with Pop and make sure he's happy...' Regan reached over and took her mother's hand and smiled fondly.

It was going to be hard without her mum to help, but they'd just have to manage somehow. Thoughts cascaded through Regan's head while she sipped her tea. She'd have to work out something for the boys when she had to go into the office. She'd have to find someone she trusted to look after them.

'Anyway, you need someone younger,' her mother said, interrupting Regan's thoughts. 'They have too much energy for me now they're growing up.'

Regan nodded. Her mother was right. Chase had had the right idea. He'd given Phoebe an idyllic childhood.

Her stomach lurched. She had to stop thinking about Chase. And besides, their situations had been completely different. He hadn't had people depending on him for their jobs. It had been just him and his daughter. In the same position, she'd probably have done exactly what he'd done. But, as it was, she'd done the best she could for everyone— her family and her employees.

'You should advertise for a live-in nanny. I'll stay here for a couple of weeks. That should give you plenty of time to find someone.'

She gave another distracted nod. She'd have to organise the advertisement straight away if she was going to manage to interview prospective nannies and select one before her mother moved out. She was already working on its wording.

'We swam with sea lions,' Cory piped up as his grand-mother helped herself to a slice of toast from the plate in the centre of the table. Her eyebrows shot up and, for the next few minutes, Will and Cory entertained her with de-scriptions of the things they'd done and seen in the short time since they'd left on Friday.

'Well,' her mother said, giving her a sideways look across the table, 'you do seem to have had a good time. And who is this Chase the boys can't stop talking about?'

Regan shrugged. 'He's just someone I met, a friend.'

Her mother smiled. 'A male friend?'

'It's not like that,' Regan said. 'We're just friends.'

And not even that any more, she thought with a painful pang.

Her mother glanced at the boys, then leaned towards her. 'If you want to have a fling, that's your business. It's about time you started living again,' she whispered behind her hand.

'Mum, please.' Regan jumped up from the table, catching her chair as it almost fell. 'You've got it wrong. There is nothing going on between me and Chase.'

She placed the chair carefully under the table. 'I'm

going to have a shower and then I'll be in my study catching up on emails.'

Her mother just smiled again and Regan wondered exactly how well her mother did know her. She'd always thought that they weren't close, but now she wasn't so sure. Her mother had touched a sore spot about Chase and Regan would have to make sure that she made it clear that the boys came first for her and always would. And that, no matter what her mum might think, she would never, *never*, have a *fling* with Chase.

Nearly two weeks later Regan grabbed the list of people she'd interviewed and mentally evaluated each one. After several minutes she tossed the list aside. Nothing wrong with any of them as far as she could see, but she couldn't imagine leaving her sons with them. If they weren't family or friends, it didn't feel right.

As a sigh escaped she slumped in her seat. What was she going to do about this child-care issue? Because she had to do something, and soon.

Will and Cory deserved better than the candidates she'd seen so far, even if they had driven her mad over the last fortnight with their constant nagging about another trip to Leo Bay.

Cory had even tried to force her hand by acting heart-broken about his favourite toy car, which he'd supposedly left at Chase's house. For a short time she'd almost been fooled, but then she'd found the car shoved beneath his mattress. Hidden, not lost, she was certain.

She shook her head. Her boys had always been so well-behaved, yet in the last couple of weeks they'd tried every trick in the book to get their own way.

Perversely, she was pleased to see how highly they thought of Chase. It confirmed her own opinion that he was wonderful with them. But it didn't alter the fact that they could never go back and how did she even begin to explain the reason?

Of course she was tempted to contact him. More than tempted. She'd lost count of the number of times she'd reached for the phone to call him, to say she wanted to see him again. Because she did. Desperately.

Repeatedly, she'd had to remind herself why she'd left. Because a relationship with Chase was a bad idea. Falling in love with a man who still loved his dead wife was a recipe for disaster. But she couldn't tell the boys the truth, so how could she possibly expect them to understand?

It wasn't as if she could say Chase was a bad person. Quite the opposite. He was kind and generous and had done a marvellous job of raising Phoebe.

Her thoughts darted all over the place as she tried to find a way through the mess. Then she jerked upright as an idea suddenly entered her head.

She was going about this child-care business all wrong. She shouldn't be looking for someone to care for the boys—she should be looking for ways she could step back from the business so she could look after them herself.

Why shouldn't she hire someone to run the business for her? As she'd told Chase, it was ticking over nicely thanks to her hard work over the last few years. Now that she'd shelved expansion plans in the short-term, why shouldn't she find someone to manage the day-to-day operations so that she could move into more of a back seat?

Her father would never had done it, she knew. But then her father had never had any time to spare for his only child, so maybe it was time to break with tradition.

She took a few deep breaths. This was a major, *major* move she was considering, but it was the right path to take. She felt it deep inside. It would be difficult to find someone she could trust to do the job well, but not as difficult as finding a nanny she could trust with her children.

And she could retain the power to approve or veto any significant changes her manager made. She'd make sure of that. She wouldn't risk the business deteriorating like it had under Jack.

With a sense of bubbling excitement in the pit of her stomach, she started to scribble notes on her pad about the type of person she'd need. She already had a dedicated farm manager—her cousin Tony, who was actively involved in the catching, feeding, health and harvesting of the tuna. She knew Tony was also keen to take over management of their environmental monitoring programme.

If she were to take a step back, what she'd need was a general manager to oversee the processing facility and work with her chief financial officer to ensure the business remained profitable. Then she'd need to do only what was essential for monitoring the existing business and developing future plans.

Deep in thought when her secretary buzzed through on the intercom, she reached for the button automatically. 'Yes, Sue?'

'You have a visitor, Regan. It's a Mr Mattner.'

She frowned at the page where the words she'd written blurred and faded. Sue couldn't be serious.

'Who?'

'A Mr Chase Mattner.' Sue cleared her throat. 'He doesn't have an appointment.'

'No, um, that's okay.' She dropped her pen and reached

up to check her hair, but then she remembered he'd seen it wet and first thing in the morning. She swallowed. 'Um, show him in, Sue, please.'

She'd been sure she was doing the right thing when she'd left him two weeks ago, but, now that he was here, all she could think about was how much she'd missed him, how her stomach was fluttering and how much she wanted to see him again.

She'd only had time to straighten her blouse before the door opened and Sue ushered Chase into her office. Regan got to her feet, her heart hammering, unsure whether to shake his hand or...

Sue let the door close behind her and walked into the office. 'Just thought I'd better mention that your next appointment, which was also your last, has cancelled. She's sick.'

'Thanks, Sue.' That was convenient since she'd just decided not to interview any more nannies. Regan moistened her lips while her secretary gave Chase a speculative stare. She couldn't help the intensely possessive feeling that buzzed through her. She was almost ready to grab Chase's arm and drag him out of there. Away from Sue.

She was *jealous*.

Heaven help her.

'*Thanks*, Sue.'

Sue looked across the office at her, one eyebrow lifting in curiosity. 'Coffee?'

Regan gave Chase a questioning glance. 'Would you like coffee?'

'Well, actually, I was hoping you might join me for lunch.'

Sue grinned. 'That works out well. I won't bother with coffee, then,' she said on her way out.

When the door had clicked shut again, Chase gave her

a wary smile. 'I'm sorry to interrupt your work. I should have called.' He darted a glance around the office. 'I was in town at a meeting. I wanted to say hi.'

'That's okay. It's a…nice surprise.'

She meant it. And when he grinned she smiled back. It *was* good to see him again.

He glanced at his watch. 'Well, perhaps we should…' He tipped his head towards the door.

She glanced at her watch. She hadn't exactly agreed to lunch but suddenly all the reasons she should say no were just out of reach. All she could think was that she wanted to talk to him, she wanted to tell him about her decision to step back from the business, she wanted to be with him if only for an hour or so.

'Yes, we should make a move,' she said before she could talk herself out of it. 'Where do you want to go?'

'Your choice.'

She swallowed. Her hands shook when she reached for the suit jacket from the back of her chair. So much for staying away from him for her own safety. He was magnetic, drawing her back. She couldn't resist him.

CHAPTER EIGHT

REGAN had chosen an Italian café on the Port Lincoln fore-shore and while they were waiting for their food to arrive she took a drink of water.

Chase studied her face. She looked tired. But then she'd also looked tired the first time he'd seen her and it hadn't stopped him wanting to get to know her. She'd been so beautiful she'd taken his breath away. Since then, though, he'd seen a relaxed and laughing Regan and he knew which he preferred. He particularly liked seeing her smile when she looked at him. He'd missed that.

She was in the shapeless suit she'd been wearing when he'd first met her, but now he knew what she looked like in a swimsuit and images of her long slim legs filled his head. He hastily pushed them back. Today was not about his reaction to her body. He hadn't only seen beneath the suit, he'd seen beneath the brisk, intelligent persona she presented to the business world, and the woman he'd found there was sweet and warm-hearted, a loving mother and his *friend*.

'How are the boys?' he asked.

'Fine, thanks. Perfectly fine.' She took another sip of water. 'How's Phoebe?'

'Fine. Really well.'

God, this was awkward. He'd agonized about what he'd say. Since he'd decided to attend the environmental protest meeting, he'd been thinking about this moment. He'd had all sorts of words ready, but now that it came to it…

He summoned a smile for the young waitress who delivered their meals. Once she'd left, he steeled himself.

'You must be wondering why I'm here.'

'Yes.' She sucked on her bottom lip for a moment, then raised her piercing blue gaze to his. 'I thought we both felt it would be better if we didn't see each other again.'

He nodded. 'But I feel bad about the way we left things. I owe you an apology.'

She waved his statement away. 'No. No, you don't. Don't let your meal go cold.'

He ate a forkful of pasta and watched her play with the salad in front of her. 'My conscience won't let me agree with you,' he said after a moment. 'It was my fault that you felt you had to leave.'

She glanced up, then back at her food. 'You don't have to do this, Chase. It was nobody's fault.'

'Hear me out, please.' He frowned, trying to summon the speech he'd prepared. In the end, he blurted, 'I loved Larissa and I was faithful to her throughout our marriage. In fact, from the day I met her until I met you, I'd never had a non-platonic thought about another woman.'

She opened her mouth as if she had something to say but, with a slight shake of her head, she closed it again.

He sucked in a deep breath before going on. 'I felt terrible about what happened out there on the cliffs.' He grimaced, reliving the guilty pangs that had racked him. 'It was like I'd had an affair right under her nose.'

She stopped shoving her salad around and pushed the

bowl away. She stared for a moment, then cleared her throat. 'I understand, Chase. You don't need to go on.'

'But I haven't finished. The thing is, Regan, as unhappy as I was at…my betrayal of Larissa, I was even more unhappy about not seeing you again.' He shrugged. 'I've hated the last two weeks. Phoebe won't shut up about you and the boys and…I've missed you. All of you.'

'Oh, Chase, stop.' Her face crumpled and she turned away. For several moments he held his breath while she appeared to be watching the passers-by on Tasman Terrace, but suddenly she looked back at him and sighed. 'I've missed you, too. But I still don't want a relationship—'

'I know, I know. Believe me, I'm not asking for that.'

Before he'd married, he'd had no trouble knowing when a woman was attracted to him. He'd learned to read the signs. But with Regan he wouldn't have been sure, if not for the memory of their brief kiss and the way her lips had instantly softened and trembled under his. As soon as he had the thought, he thrust it away again. He didn't want a relationship any more than Regan did.

'I promise that nothing of the kind will happen again. I won't do anything that might spoil what we have.' He leaned forward, resting his elbows on the table. 'Can we try again to be friends?'

Regan hesitated. 'What if we can't? There are other people involved. Three of them. The children. If we're friends one day and not the next, they'll be confused and upset.'

'Yes, I'm aware of that and it's partly for their sakes that I believe we should try. They were happy when we were all together.' He gave her a sheepish smile. 'Phoebe knows I planned to see you today. Please don't disappoint her, Regan.'

Regan narrowed her eyes.

He swallowed, waiting. She'd be within her rights to be cross with him for that. He'd deserve it.

'What you mean is, don't make you look bad,' she said.

He nodded.

'I don't want the boys to get any ideas about us becoming a family.'

'So we make it clear that we're just friends.'

She heaved a sigh that seemed to be dragged from her toes. 'I lied earlier—when I said the boys were fine. They're not fine; they're driving me mad with questions about when they can come and see you again.'

He grinned before he could stop himself. 'I'm sorry. That must be very annoying.'

'You have no idea. Actually, it's been an eventful couple of weeks.'

She told him about her mother's decision, her unsuccessful search for a nanny and her resolution to hand over the running of the business to a manager. Nothing had changed, she thought with a wry smile. She still told him everything without hesitation, as if her mouth had a mind of its own when he was around.

'When do the boys go back to school?'

'In another week and a half. Why?'

'They could come back to Leo Bay with me and stay till the end of the holidays. That would give you more time to focus on finding the right person. And you could join us for the weekends. What about it?'

He held his breath, willing her to agree. When, after another deep sigh, she nodded, he reached instinctively for her hand.

'They'll be so happy,' she said.

'Of course they will. But they'll miss you. Is there any chance you could make the weekends long ones?'

Her gaze slid away, then snapped back. 'Try and stop me.'

Relieved that she hadn't pulled away her hand, he ran his thumb across the back of it. The feel of her soft skin sent sensations zinging along his nerves. Sensations that reminded him what he'd promised and he quickly let go.

'It feels good to have everything out in the open,' he said. 'You don't know how pleased I am that I came to see you.'

The waitress arrived to collect their plates. 'Would you like a coffee or something?' she asked with a flirty smile in his direction.

He looked at Regan and she shook her head. 'I think I need some fresh air.'

'No, thanks. We've finished,' he said to the girl and got to his feet.

Regan stood up from the table. He'd made a promise and she felt sure he'd keep it. That was why she'd agreed to give their friendship another go. For one perverse instant she wished he hadn't promised, but she gave herself a mental slap. A hard one. The last thing—the *very* last thing—she wanted was a romantic relationship which could only end in heartbreak. This way, she got to keep Chase as a friend and neither she nor the boys would get hurt.

It was perfect. But the fact remained that when he'd touched her hand sensations had bubbled through her veins and made her want more. Much more.

But, if she avoided skin contact, she could do this, and she was glad she'd agreed. There was the benefit of solving the child-care issue, of course, but, in truth, she wanted to go back to Leo Bay every bit as much as her sons did. She'd been happy there. Happier than she'd ever been before and she wanted to recapture the feeling. Will and Cory would be thrilled when she gave them the news.

She swung her handbag on to her shoulder and smiled at Chase as she moved towards the door. His tension at the beginning of lunch had been palpable and she'd ached for him. It couldn't have been easy to talk about Larissa the way he had and to lay out his feelings about their kiss.

She cared about him. She wouldn't deny it. It had twisted her insides when he'd forced himself to open up. She took a deep breath and lifted her face into the sea breeze. The sun was scorching hot, as always at this time of year, but the rush of cool air across her skin felt good. They soon reached the end of the jetty and she grasped the smooth metal rail with her free hand as she leaned forward to stare into the depths.

'See anything?' Chase asked.

'Bait fish, that's all.' Smiling, she turned to face him, leaning her hip against the rail. 'Can we swim with the sea lions again this weekend?'

'Anything you want to do. It was great to see you enjoying yourself so much.'

'They're so cute. So playful.'

He nodded. 'Jan will be pleased to see you as well.'

She smiled. 'What time do you want to leave? I have to go back to the office. I'll need to tidy up some loose ends before I go home to get the boys ready. And this time I plan to pack some clothes for myself.'

'Well, I have something to do too so I'll meet you at your house in a couple of hours, if that suits you.'

She nodded and gave him the address. 'You really came to Port Lincoln for a meeting?'

'Yes, but that was this morning.' He grinned. 'What I'm going to do now is a surprise, but you'll see soon enough.'

Later, while Will and Cory piled into Chase's car, Regan told her mother again that she and Chase were just friends.

Her mother fluffed up her short hair. 'Goodness, I couldn't blame you if you did have a fling with him. He's a nice-looking man.'

'And a *nice* man. He's a widower so there's no chance of a *fling*. Besides, I would never put the boys at risk of being hurt again.'

'You surely don't think they remember their father walking out, do you, Regan? They were too young.'

'Yes, but they know they don't have a daddy they can see. They know he never gets in touch with them, even for birthdays or Christmas. Don't you think that hurts them?'

'Yes, of course. I'm sure you know what you're doing, Regan. You never listened to me anyway.'

'Mum! How can you say that?'

'It's true. You never listened to anyone but your father and, once he'd gone, you expected Jack to take his place.' She grimaced. 'He was never going to be able to do that, was he? So, after he disappeared, you made all the decisions by yourself. You've never asked anyone's advice since Jack left, nor listened to anyone's opinion.'

Regan shook her head. What her mum said was true, but it wasn't because she wouldn't listen. It was because there *was* no one else to make the decisions—about the business or about her family. Everyone expected her to know what to do.

She bent forward to kiss her mother's cheek. 'I tried to do my best for everyone, Mum. I'm sorry if that hurt you.

I'll miss you while you are with Pop. Take care of yourself, won't you?'

Her mother laid a hand on Regan's cheek but, before she could answer, Chase strode towards them. He lifted one of the bags she'd packed and there was a clunk as he straightened. He gave her a questioning look.

'It's just some food and household stuff,' she said with a dismissive wave.

'But—'

'I couldn't land you with all of us again and not contribute. It wouldn't be right.'

He shook his head but he was smiling. 'I can afford to feed us all, Regan.'

'And it would make me happy to help out.'

'Okay.' He picked up the rest of the bags and nodded at Regan's mother. 'It was nice to meet you.'

Regan gave her a hug. 'Give Pop my love.'

'I will. I'll miss you, too, Regan, but I'll be back for a visit before long.'

'You'd better.'

As they separated, her mother reached up and touched her cheek again. 'I hope he makes you happy, Regan. You deserve it.'

Regan frowned. She thought she'd made the situation clear, but just then an excited yell from the car made her turn to see Will waving her over. 'I have to go, Mum. Take care.'

She hurried to the car. 'What is it, Will?'

'Look what Chase has got for us.' He pointed into a cardboard box on the back seat between him and his brother. 'It's a puppy!'

Regan shot a horrified glance at Chase.

'*Us* being all of us,' he said quickly. 'He'll live with Phoebe and me but Will and Cory can help to look after him when they come to stay. Sound fair?'

Regan gave a reluctant nod while the boys voiced their agreement loudly. It sounded fair since it would get the boys off her back about acquiring a dog. The problem was, if she and Chase parted ways again for whatever reason, this innocent puppy would be one more source of heartbreak for her sons.

Her jaw stiffened as she made her way to the front passenger seat. They couldn't mess up. They had to stick to their friendship pact. It was the only way to ensure no one ended up hurt.

Giggling came from the back seat as Chase started the car and set off. Curious, Regan twisted around and peered through the gap between the seats.

'What type of dog is it?' she asked.

'A Labradoodle. They don't drop hair, or so I'm told. Hence, less work. It's a cross between a Labrador and a poodle.'

'You'll have to be careful not to lose it on the beach,' she said. 'It's the same colour as the sand.'

When the boys laughed she felt an easing of the tension in her shoulders. They wouldn't mess up again. What they had was too good to lose. Her mother's parting comment slipped back into her thoughts. If the boys were happy, she'd be happy. That was all she needed.

The journey passed quickly and much more noisily than the last time she'd driven them this way. As Regan got out of the car, Phoebe ran into her arms and she picked her up, hugged her to her shoulder and realised how much she'd missed the little girl. Then she looked at Jan, who'd walked up behind Phoebe.

'Good to see you again, Regan.'

The genuine warmth of Jan's smile touched Regan and she smiled back. 'You, too, Jan.'

Chase joined them, kissed his daughter, then moved away to open the rear door of his four-wheel drive, letting out Will, Cory and the puppy. Phoebe was soon on the ground and joining in the noise and excitement.

'Cute.' Jan petted the puppy, said hello to the boys, then left with a promise that she'd bring over the two fishing rods she'd found for them.

Regan followed Chase into the house. The first time she'd come here it had all seemed very strange, but this time, as she looked around at the mismatched furniture, she felt welcome.

She dropped her handbag on the floor, flopped down on one of the squishy sofas and kicked off her shoes. Fanciful, she knew, but it felt like coming home—more so than arriving at her own smartly decorated house had ever felt.

'You have a very comfortable place here,' she said as Chase reappeared from depositing their bags in the bedrooms. 'It's a real home.'

'Thanks. I think so, too.'

'Did you have holidays here with Larissa?'

'No. We never got around to it. On the rare occasions we had annual leave at the same time, we went to Fiji or Bali. I suppose, if Larissa had lived, we'd have brought the children here for summer holidays.'

His face clouded and she guessed it was at the word *children*. He'd probably hoped to have more than one.

'I'm glad we didn't stay here or I would have been

seeing her wherever I looked. I left the city to get away from all that.'

He bent to scoop up the puppy, which had found its way inside and he held it in one hand while its three pursuers crowded round him. 'We need to find a name for this little one,' he said. 'So why don't we all have a cold drink and talk about it?'

Later, when the puppy had been formally named Deefer—D for Dog being the limit of Phoebe's alphabet learning—and the children had disappeared into the back garden, Regan sighed.

'How did you get to be so good at being a parent?'

In the middle of gathering plastic cups from the coffee table, Chase looked up, startled. 'Me? You're kidding, aren't you?'

'No, I'm not kidding. They all adore you.'

Chase straightened, leaving the cups on the table. 'I don't know.' With a serious expression, he moved to sit next to her on the sofa. 'I bought a dog. I suppose I'm bound to be popular right now.'

She shook her head. 'It's more than that. Did you learn from your own parents? What are they like?'

He gave a low chuckle. 'I definitely did not. And they're…eccentric.'

'Eccentric? Really?' Her eyes widened. 'Are they still alive?'

'Yes. Don't ask me where exactly. Last time I heard, they were in the Himalayas but they could be anywhere now. I think Cambodia was on the agenda. Or it might have been Laos.'

'Goodness. They must be well-off if they can afford to travel so much.'

'They are. Disgustingly.' He combined a shrug with a rueful smile. 'But you wouldn't know it to look at them.'

'Well, they can't be too eccentric, they made sure you had a good education, didn't they?'

He nodded. 'It was convenient for them to do so. They put me in boarding school and forgot about me.'

His tone was light but she felt an undercurrent of something more serious.

'What do you mean?'

'Exactly what I said. They forgot about me. When the holidays came around, they were too busy having adventures to remember me. Other kids went home. If I was lucky, I went to stay with one of them.'

'Oh, goodness.' Her heart ached for the boy he'd been.

'And even when my parents were around, they weren't really *there*. They were busy planning their next trip.' Shrugging, he said, 'Don't worry, I'm not traumatised by the memory.'

He grinned but she'd seen enough of him to know this grin wasn't as broad as normal and his eyes dropped before her gaze.

'What does bother me is that they have no interest in getting to know Phoebe. I would have appreciated their help with her after Larissa died, but they didn't want anything to do with her.' His face twisted. 'I don't need assistance from them now, but they're Phoebe's only living grandparents. I wish…' He let his words trail off with a shake of his head.

She felt his pain. She understood. This time, it was she who reached for and held his hand.

'That's something else we have in common,' she said. 'Parents who didn't have much time for us.'

It hurt her to say it and her chest tightened even more when Chase gave her a sympathetic look.

'But you must have resolved your issues. At least with your mother. You seem to get on well enough.'

'Mum's always been around but we've never been... close. We might as well have been flatmates.'

He tilted his head. 'And your father?'

'He was always too—' Her voice broke and a sob came out instead of the words she'd meant to say. 'I'm sorry.' She wiped tears from her eyes with the back of her hand. 'This is ridiculous. It was years ago.'

But the more she wiped, the more the tears flowed. She felt Chase's weight lift from the sofa and then he was back, pushing a box of tissues into her hands. She thanked him and mopped at her face with a tightly bunched wad. After a while, the tears slowed and the sobs eased off.

'God, I'm glad no one saw that,' she said before blowing her nose. 'I mean, no one but you.' She glanced at him. Strangely, she didn't mind that he'd seen her cry. If it had been anyone else she'd have been terribly embarrassed that she'd lost control. 'I must look awful.'

He surprised a smile from her by grimacing. 'Yes. Scary.'

'I don't know why I did that. All I was going to say was that my father was always too busy with work to have time for me.' She swallowed a further sob that tried to escape. 'See? No big deal.'

Chase nodded slowly. 'I imagine you've kept that bottled up for a long time.'

She opened her mouth to argue but then nodded and murmured, 'Maybe. I think my whole life until he died was about needing his approval, and I never really had it.'

'Oh, Regan.'

She shrugged. 'It's okay. He wanted a pretty little girl and he got me—a great gawky lump of a daughter.'

Chase reached out and smoothed back her hair, pushing it behind her ear, his fingertips trailing down her jaw to her chin. It was such a tender, comforting touch and it made her sigh softly.

'Well, you showed him, didn't you?'

She swallowed. 'I wasn't fishing for compliments. I know I'm not pretty.'

His eyes widened. 'I wouldn't use the word *pretty* either.'

'No, I know.' So when he'd told her she was beautiful on the boat—what was that about?

'*Pretty* doesn't do you justice at all. Stunning, I'd have said.'

She stared. Stunning? She cleared her throat. 'As I said, I wasn't what my father wanted, and I get that. I understand.'

He tilted his head. 'But it hurts to know you weren't the most important person in your parents' life, doesn't it?'

She nodded.

'I make light of my childhood,' he went on, 'but I'm not as blasé about it as I appear. Not when I remember how much it hurt at the time.'

She laced her fingers with his. 'At least we're both trying to do better for our own children.' She shrugged and sniffed. 'We're not letting history repeat itself.'

He pulled her into his arms. It felt so good to be held by him. Safe. Secure. She forgot the reasons why she shouldn't relax against him and did it anyway.

'I hate that you didn't have a happy childhood.' He stroked her hair as he spoke. 'I wish I could change that.'

She laughed against his shoulder, then pulled herself

together enough to move back out of his hold. 'You can't but, honestly, it's fine. I don't know why I cried. It's not like me at all. I think I must be a bit run-down and it's making me more emotional than normal.'

'Well, I *can* do something about *that*. Consider yourself on holiday as of now. When do you intend to go back to Port Lincoln?'

'Monday night.'

'Right. Between now and Monday night, you are going to be pampered, waited on and spoilt so much that you'll go back to work full of energy.'

She laughed. 'Don't be ridiculous. If I wanted that, I'd have gone to a health spa.'

'I'm serious. And, to start with, put your feet up here.' He moved along the sofa and patted his thigh.

'Put my feet in your lap? You must be joking.'

'Do it.'

'No.'

With an exaggerated sigh, he reached for her legs and, almost before she realised what he was doing, he spun her around and settled her bare feet in his lap.

'What are you doing?' She giggled as she tried to pull her feet away.

'Giving you a foot rub.' He held on to her ankles until she stopped struggling. 'Relax. That's what this weekend is all about from now on.'

His thumbs moved in circles against the balls of her feet. She moaned, then leaned back against the arm of the sofa and closed her eyes.

When, several minutes later, she opened them again, he was watching her face.

'How does that feel?'

'Like heaven. I didn't know my feet ached so much. It's not as if I have a job that involves lots of standing.'

'Probably a reflection of the tension in the rest of your body.'

She lifted an eyebrow. 'And how would you know so much about it? You're not a closet reflexologist or something, are you?'

'Or something.' He dropped his gaze. 'When Larissa was sick, she liked me to rub her feet. She said it relaxed her.' She saw him swallow. 'It was one of the few things I could do for her.'

As she watched, a small smile curved his lips and his eyes softened. Larissa, she thought. He was remembering Larissa.

'What are you thinking about?' she asked gently.

He looked up, still smiling, but his eyes were wary. 'You don't want to know.'

'Yes, I do. Really.'

With a little shrug, he said, 'I was thinking that you have beautiful legs.'

Regan gasped. 'I thought…'

'I told you that you didn't want to know.'

She didn't get a chance to respond because the sliding door opened and the three children rushed in, as did Deefer.

'We're hungry,' Phoebe called. 'So's Deefer. Can we give him some food?'

'We'd better do that,' Chase said. 'But first I want you all to do something for me.'

Regan curled her feet beneath her and covered her legs with her long skirt.

'What, Daddy?'

Phoebe climbed into his lap while Will and Cory came to stand close.

'I want to make sure that Regan—your mum,' he said, nodding to the boys, 'has a really good rest while she's here. She's been working hard and she's very tired.'

Regan smiled and shook her head when all three small faces looked at her. 'I'm fine. Really.'

Ignoring Regan's comment, Chase said, 'We're going to pamper her this weekend.'

'What does pamper mean, Daddy?'

'It means we're not going to let Regan do anything for herself if we can do it for her.'

'Okay.'

'So who's going to help me cook dinner?'

Regan was the only volunteer whose help wasn't accepted and she sat back on the sofa feeling a little strange. She couldn't remember the last time she'd had nothing to do.

A moment later, Will appeared at her side. 'Chase told me to give you these.'

She took the pile of books from him and smiled. 'Just what I need. Thanks.'

Almost shyly, he wound his arms around her neck and gave her a clumsy hug. 'I'm sorry you're tired, Mum. I hope you feel better soon. You're the best.'

'I'm fine, Will, honestly. But thank you.' She had to blink rapidly before he pulled away so he wouldn't see the tears that had sprung to her eyes.

CHAPTER NINE

WHEN the children were settled in bed and Chase picked up two wineglasses, Regan said, 'Are we going out to watch the sun set?'

'Unless there's something else you'd rather do?'

She shook her head. She felt more relaxed than she could remember and she could think of nothing better than watching the sky change with Chase. 'I hope I don't fall asleep this time.'

'It's okay if you do. I don't mind carrying you to bed.' He looked up from pouring the wine, his expression apologetic. 'I meant—'

'It's all right. I know you meant that in a purely platonic way.' She held out her hand for one of the glasses and, when he passed it to her, she walked to the front door. 'Don't be long,' she called over her shoulder, 'it's already starting.'

They'd just settled on the bench when Jan turned into the driveway.

'Hi, guys. I forgot to ask you, Chase, how the meeting went this morning.'

'It went well. I think there's a case for an injunction. The area is awaiting marine national park status from one government department and another department has allowed the development to proceed based on a rushed application that was not properly scrutinised.'

He paused for a moment and Regan turned to look at him. Frowning while he considered the problem, his face was serious and so close. She wanted to touch the vertical creases between his eyes, to trace the ones radiating from the corners of his eyes and smooth the lines near his mouth.

'I believe we could show that the farm will not be ecologically sustainable,' he went on. 'Even if we can't get the approval thrown out, we can probably hold up the process long enough for the marine park to be established.'

'Okay. Good to hear. I won't disturb your evening any longer.'

'Sure. See you tomorrow.'

Jan waved as she headed back to her own house and Regan twisted to look into his eyes. Her face was only a short distance from his and she'd never felt so close to anyone—both physically and emotionally. 'So what was that about? What farm?'

He hesitated. 'An operator wants to locate a fish farm near the bay.'

His gaze dropped to her mouth and her stomach lurched. She held her breath as he edged a little closer. Her lips tingled in anticipation. She wanted him to kiss her. The knowledge terrified her but she wanted it badly.

Then she registered what he'd said. 'A fish farm? What's the problem with that?'

After a moment's hesitation he sucked in a breath and pulled back. 'Nothing wrong with fish farming *per se*. The problem with this particular one is that it's to be located only three kilometres from the sea lion breeding colony.'

'And?'

'It shouldn't have been given the go-ahead. The inevitable result is that sea lions will be maimed or hurt.'

She winced. 'I don't like the sound of that.'

'No. Science, history and common sense all say this is a bad, bad move. But don't worry. Like I said to Jan, we'll probably get an injunction.'

It wasn't the right moment to mention that she'd considered locating a farm near the bay at one time. She hadn't gone ahead with it and now she never would.

'Have you given any more thought to becoming an environmental lawyer?'

He nodded. 'I'm thinking about it.' Then he looked away. 'Hey, it's dark.'

'So it is. Did you see the sun set?'

'No.'

'Me neither.'

'Are you cold? Do you want to go inside?'

'No, and no. I'd like to stay right here.'

Regan knew Chase had wanted to kiss her. He'd resisted and she was grateful to him for that. She guessed that he too would be glad that he hadn't given in to the moment.

They could do this. They could overcome this attraction between them and focus on their friendship because that was so much more important.

She settled into a comfortable position and they sat in a companionable silence, sipping wine, not needing to talk.

Regan thought back to their earlier conversation about their parents. She'd spent years seeking her father's approval. Even after his death, she'd chosen her path based on what he would have wanted. She hadn't sold the business. She'd worked her butt off to make it a success for her children so that her father's dream of passing it on to his grandsons could be realised.

But, if she'd had her choice, what would she have done with her life?

She'd been an ordinary girl, not particularly interested in a career. She'd only studied because it had been expected of her. All she'd wanted was to be a mum and to be married to a man who loved her.

So no, she wouldn't have chosen the direction her life had taken to this point, but now, finally, things were looking up. If everything went to plan, she'd soon be able to be a full-time mum and her kids weren't too old to need her.

And, for tonight, she couldn't imagine being anywhere else. She was right where she wanted to be.

Regan woke in Phoebe's bed, alone except for a small, warm, furry body curled up behind her knees. She had a clear recollection of getting into bed this time.

A childish giggle outside the door caught her attention. There were more giggles and then a very adult knock.

'Come in.' She scrambled to sit up, disturbing Deefer, who climbed into her lap and settled down again.

'There he is,' Chase said when he opened the door. 'Sorry.'

She looked down at the puppy she was patting. 'No problem. I like him.'

'And it looks like the feeling's mutual.' Chase held the door ajar and Will entered the bedroom, followed by Cory and Phoebe.

'We brought you breakfast in bed,' Phoebe said in a loud voice. 'And I picked some special flowers because you're special.'

She gasped. 'Thank you.'

Deefer moved with a little encouragement and she helped Will to settle the tray on her lap.

'There was no need to go to so much trouble.' She looked at Chase and he held up his hands in a gesture of denial.

She pressed a hand to her chest. 'Whose idea was this?'

'Mine,' Cory said. 'Do you like it?'

'Of course I do,' she said. 'It's lovely.'

Cory hugged her neck. 'I'm glad, Mummy.'

'I made toast,' Will said. 'But Chase *supervised*.' He glanced at Chase as if they shared a private joke.

Chase gave him an indulgent smile, then lifted his gaze to meet hers and his smile grew broader. 'How do you feel this morning?'

Her stomach fluttered and she clamped down on the ill-timed, inappropriate reaction. 'Very well, thanks.'

'That's good to hear. I saw Jan this morning when I went to borrow some honey—'

'It's nice honey, Mum,' Cory cut in.

'And I've arranged for us to go out on the *Explorer* this morning.'

She grinned at the boys and they jumped with excitement.

'And Jan wants to know if the children can go fishing again this afternoon.'

A whole afternoon alone with him. She wasn't sure about that. Look what had happened the last time they'd tried it.

'Sure,' she managed. 'Even better, why don't we all go fishing?'

'*Yay!*'

She grinned at the boys' reaction. She'd discovered that she liked to surprise them more than almost anything.

'Good. Come on.' Chase ushered the children out of the room. 'And take Deefer outside,' he called after them.

Pushing the door shut, he came back to the bed with an intent look. 'You don't have to avoid being alone with me,' he said. 'You can trust me. I swear.'

But could she trust herself?

'I just think it's easier this way,' she said with a gentle smile. 'Besides, I'd like to learn how to fish.'

'Right.' He rubbed his jaw and looked sceptical. 'I can see how you'd be longing to handle wriggling maggots and slimy cockles.'

Her face twisted in distaste.

He chuckled and his eyes glittered as he turned away. 'See you after breakfast.'

Regan wouldn't have thought it possible, but she had even more fun with the sea lions than she'd had the first time. It wasn't that they were any more playful than on their previous meeting, but rather that she was willing to relax and let things happen, more than she ever had before.

She felt no need to control the situation and this feeling overflowed into the trip back to shore. She laughed with Jan, teased Mike and Chase and had the children in fits of giggles. It was wonderful to spend time with Chase, safe in the knowledge that they both knew the parameters of their relationship.

Later, when they were on their way out into the bay again, this time with the boat loaded down with fishing tackle and, to Regan's disgust, buckets of bait, she wondered what she'd let herself in for. She could have spent the afternoon with her feet up, reading. But one look at the smiles on her sons' faces convinced her she'd made the right choice.

Mike anchored the *Explorer*. 'This is a likely spot,' he said as he joined the rest of them.

'How do you know?' she asked, gazing at the water. 'It looks the same as the rest of the bay.'

'The electronic fish finder says so,' Mike drawled.

'Ah.' Regan picked up the rod she'd been given and watched as the others dug into buckets and baited their hooks. Even Phoebe flipped open a cockle shell like an expert.

'Need a hand?'

Chase's voice at her side made her jump.

'No, of course not. I run a fish farm, for goodness' sake.'

'From a desk.'

She frowned and reached into the bucket of cockles. 'I can do this.' Opening the shell the way she'd seen Phoebe do it, she looked at its contents. 'On second thoughts…' She gave Chase a sheepish smile. 'Yes, please.'

Laughing, he took the cockle from her and made quick work of baiting her hook. 'Now, do you know how to cast?'

She shook her head.

'Hold the rod in your right hand.' He moved to the side of the boat and she followed. 'Release the brake on the reel with your left hand, but keep the thumb of your right hand on the line to stop it spooling out.'

She looked at him blankly. 'What?'

He grinned. 'Here.' He stood behind her and reached around to cover her right hand with his.

Only their hands touched but she was totally aware of his body so close…she'd only have to lean back a little and…

Heat rushed to her face. And she'd thought going fishing was the easier option?

She felt his voice in her ear, but had to ask him to repeat the words. He spoke again, patiently explaining what to do, then he moved her thumb, pressing it against the reel. It felt so intimate, and yet she knew that wasn't deliberate on his part. He'd probably given exactly the same matter-of-fact lesson to the children.

'That will stop the line falling off the reel when you release the brake, like this.'

He flipped back part of the reel. 'Now, bring back the rod—taking care not to hook anyone else—and flick it forward, letting go of the line at the same time.'

He matched his actions to his words and she watched her hook fly through the air, then drop into the water with a plop.

'Let the hook sink a little way, then apply the brake.'

She clicked the brake into place and at the same time Chase let go of her rod and moved to her side. She let out the breath she'd been holding.

'That's all there is to it,' he said.

'Great. Thanks. What do I do now?'

'Wait. And, if you're really lucky, nothing will happen.'

She laughed. 'How will I know if something *does* happen?'

'You'll feel a tug on your line.' He smiled and his eyes lingered on hers for a long moment. Suddenly he reached out and adjusted the peak of the baseball cap she was wearing, letting his fingertips trail lightly across her cheek as he said, 'Don't get burnt, beautiful.'

She bit her lip as he walked away. *Damn* him. Why couldn't he have been…different? Anything but what he was—the most wonderful man she'd ever met.

Back at the house, Regan couldn't shake the grin from her face while the children chattered about their fishing trip. She was the only one who hadn't caught a thing, and she was perfectly satisfied.

'You don't look so tired now, Mum. Did you have a good time fishing?'

She looked down at Will and on impulse dragged him into a tight hug.

'*Mum!* You're squishing me.'

'Sorry.' Releasing him with a rueful smile, she said, 'I had a lovely afternoon.'

'Well, it looks like we have fish for tea so I'd better make a start,' Chase said. 'I need volunteers to help in the kitchen.'

Regan didn't bother to volunteer. She knew she'd be refused and for once she was quite happy to stretch out on the sofa like a cat and luxuriate in doing nothing. She enjoyed all this—the experience of being part of a family. Even if it wasn't for real, it was the next best thing and she loved it.

After a moment, Deefer jumped on to the sofa and snuggled into the crook of her arm. Phoebe came to take him away.

'No, it's okay, sweetie. He can stay.'

Phoebe went off to the kitchen and Regan settled back, stroking the puppy with one hand. It was almost like having a small baby again. A sudden uninvited image flashed into her mind—of having Chase's baby. The idea made her stomach quiver and her chest tighten. It was ridiculous. She shook her head to wipe out the thought. She didn't know where it had come from.

One thing she did know, though, was that if she'd had Chase's child, it would have had a loving, caring father. Not like Will and Cory.

A tear trickled from the corner of her eye.

After they'd eaten they went down to the beach and Chase showed Will and Cory how to skim pebbles across the surface of the water. He demonstrated to Will how to angle his wrist so he could make his pebble go further and stood back to watch his attempt.

'Not bad,' he said as he saw the stone enter the water. 'Definite improvement.'

Will went off to find another pebble and Chase turned to gaze at Regan and Phoebe, who were collecting shells. He heard Regan exclaim over a shell that Phoebe held out to her and his chest felt heavy.

With the breeze billowing her loose skirt and her bare feet, she looked so different from the way she'd appeared when he'd first seen her—and even more beautiful.

His chest ached from a couple of days of roller coaster emotions. So much for his simple, straightforward life. It had suddenly become very complicated.

He'd never forget sitting alongside Regan while she wept over the pain of her childhood. She had no idea how her tears had affected him. If he never saw her cry again it would be too soon.

And then today, witnessing her frank joy following their morning swim had made his heart swell.

Watching her now as she shared with his daughter the excitement of finding treasure on the beach, he couldn't explain how he felt. He just knew that every aspect of her had an effect on him that no other woman had ever had.

Even Larissa.

He dug his heels into the damp sand. It was a hell of an admission, but he'd never felt this incredible connection with Larissa. He'd loved her, but he hadn't been kicked in the gut by a bewildering mix of emotions whenever he'd looked at her.

He glanced up again, drawn by the sound of female

laughter. Panic churned his stomach at the sight of Regan swinging Phoebe in circles. Panic that the way he felt about Regan was spinning out of his control.

He was afraid.

As Larissa had lain dying, he'd sworn that no one would take her place. When she'd shaken her head and told him she wanted him to find someone else, he'd refused to listen.

Regan was as different from Larissa as it was possible to be. She wouldn't take Larissa's place, but she certainly seemed to be carving out a place of her own in his heart.

This…thing that was happening to him was bigger than either his vow to Larissa or his promise to Regan. His only hope was to keep it hidden, because if he let Regan have a glimpse of the direction his feelings were taking she'd leave.

And he was sure that if she left again it would be a disaster for him.

CHAPTER TEN

FOR Regan the long weekend had been idyllic. Chase had convinced her to put her faith in his tiny aluminium boat and they'd all explored the tucked away beaches and tiny bays of what she now understood to be an inlet of the Southern Ocean.

They'd taken a picnic basket and spent hours wandering from beach to beach, playing games with the children and finally coming back to the house to curl up together, all five—six, counting Deefer—on one sofa, watching animated movies that she'd never had the time before to share with the boys.

Life did not get any better, she'd decided, and leaving on Monday evening had been a real wrench. Still, she'd done it and, as Chase had predicted, she'd been revitalised when she'd entered the office on Tuesday morning.

Within the first few hours she'd written up a detailed job specification for a general manager and commissioned an employment agency to begin the search.

By Friday she had the agency's short-list and was ready to start interviewing, but she was also desperate to return to Leo Bay. She was missing Chase, the boys, Phoebe and even Deefer. She longed to see them all again, but now she had something else on her mind.

She closed the file she'd been working on and took a letter from her top drawer. She'd read the letter before—numerous times. But she smoothed out the single page and scanned the words again.

And again her chest squeezed tight at the impact of those words.

Jack.

In Australia.

Asking to see Will and Cory.

Her gut instinct told her to refuse. What right did he have to come here unsettling them? He'd given up all his rights when he'd walked out.

But then her brain took over from her gut and said she couldn't in all fairness keep him from seeing the boys. They were his flesh and blood. And, more to the point, *they* would want to see *him*.

But how much control did she have over this? Could she insist on being present at all times? How could she minimise the emotional fallout from the meeting?

She needed to know what Jack's legal entitlements were before she started imposing restrictions on his access. She needed to talk to a lawyer or at least someone who could advise her, and Chase was the obvious person. As her friend, he'd have her interests at heart, and he also cared about the boys, but she believed he'd still be able to offer an impartial assessment of the situation.

Dropping her head into her hands, she wondered how she'd get through this. Quite apart from the effect on Will and Cory, which worried her immensely, there were her own feelings. She'd loved him once. Would seeing him again re-awaken feelings that had been long buried?

* * *

Regan drove to Leo Bay in a daze. Once she'd parked in the driveway she could scarcely remember the details of the journey and the admission shook her. She took several deep, steadying breaths before opening the door of the car. By this time she'd been spotted and the children streamed out of the house to give her a group hug, while Deefer yelped and sniffed at her feet.

Eventually the children tired of the hugs and ran back inside to continue their games. Regan blew out a breath as she met Chase's gaze.

'Oh, boy, am I glad to be back,' she said.

'Difficult week?'

'It was a good week, actually. Until today.'

'What happened today?'

She looked past him to where Cory was lining up toy cars on the front bench. 'Something I want to talk to you about. Later.'

He reached into the car for her bag, then closed the door. 'How did it go with the employment agencies?'

'Fine. I already have a short-list of candidates to start interviewing after the weekend.'

'Excellent work. Listen, Jan suggested the kids could sleep over at her house one night this weekend while Mike's away. I haven't mentioned it to them yet; I wanted to wait and see what you thought of the idea.'

'Why?' She squinted up at him.

'We could drive up the coast for some of those famous oysters and some adult conversation over dinner.'

Just what she needed. 'Not that I want to be rid of them, but how soon can she take them?'

'She said any time.'

'Tonight?'

He nodded. 'I guess so.'

She saw surprise flit across his face but she was too wound up to do or say anything else before she headed for the house.

The children's excitement when Jan came to collect them gave Regan a heart-wrenching pang of guilt. They thought they were being granted a special night out when really she wanted them out of the way so she could talk about the boys' father.

She mustn't think that way. All three children *would* have a special night; Jan would see to it. Regan had no doubt that Jan adored all the children.

When the house was quiet again—even Deefer had been packed off to Jan's house—Regan went back into the bedroom she shared with Phoebe and sorted through the clothes in her bag. She was glad she'd brought a nice skirt. Holding it up to her body, she checked her reflection. It was shorter and tighter than any other she owned.

Normally, she wore loose clothes that disguised her long thin legs and made her feel less like a giraffe. She'd had no inkling that they'd be going out when she'd packed this skirt but had tossed it into the bag because it made her feel feminine. And she didn't want to analyse why on earth *that* was important.

To go with the red skirt, she had some red canvas espadrilles which, while still casual, would look dressier than her usual flat sandals, and a sleeveless white top with a cute lace insert across the low-cut neckline.

She'd even bought some new lacy underwear...but Chase wouldn't know about that. Just the thought of him looking at her body in her underwear sent ripples of desire through her and she took a deep breath to calm down.

Gathering her things together, she headed for the bathroom. Chase was nowhere to be seen but she guessed he'd be busy outside. Fixing something. He was good at that.

She'd just finished drying her hair when she heard a knock on the bedroom door. It had to be Chase. His timing, as always, was perfect. She opened the door. His timing wasn't the only thing that was perfect about him; there was also…well, everything.

And when his warm honey-brown eyes looked her over, she thought she was going to melt.

'God, Regan, you look gorgeous. And you look about eighteen. Are you sure you're a mother of two? I feel like I should ask your parents for permission to take you out.'

She smiled. 'But this isn't a date so you don't need permission.' She touched her face. 'I should have brought some make-up. I didn't know we'd be going out.'

'You don't need it. You look fantastic without it.' He held her gaze for a long moment, then let out a long breath. 'Are you ready to go?'

Her mouth had dried, she realised, and she gave herself a mental shake to start her brain functioning again. 'Sure.'

In the restaurant a little later, seated at a window that opened on to wide timber decking with a view of the ocean beyond, Regan laughed at Chase's storytelling while she ate oysters. The way he told it, the few days he'd had the three children to himself had been unremitting chaos, relieved only by a few hours of sleep each night.

She knew it was a huge exaggeration for her benefit, to make her feel missed and needed. And she appreciated his efforts.

'You wanted to talk about something,' Chase prompted gently.

'Yes.' She reached down to her bag, pulled out Jack's letter and opened it again. This time she didn't read it. She handed it to Chase. 'What do you think of this?'

She saw his face darken as he read. When he looked up, he said, 'More to the point, what do *you* think of it?'

'I'm having difficulty accepting that it's real.'

He rubbed the paper between his thumb and finger. 'It's real.'

She sighed. 'Does he have the right to see the boys? Legally, I mean.'

'I gather he didn't ask for custody at the time of the divorce?'

She shook her head. 'He had legal representation in court but no, he didn't ask for anything, so I thought that was the end of it.'

'He could go to court now and he'd be granted visitation rights. The courts take fathers' rights very seriously today because of a perceived imbalance in the past.'

This confirmed what she'd suspected.

'But the Family Court would frown on the fact that he's had no contact in five years so he'd struggle to get more than these rights. And if you could prove that he's an unfit parent and the boys would be in danger with him, the Court would only grant limited access and supervised visits.'

Jack wouldn't hurt the boys—not physically. She was sure of that. She answered Chase's questioning look with another headshake.

'Or, if you think there's a risk he'd try to take them out of the country, the Court would again insist on supervised access.'

She stared through the window for a few seconds while she thought about this possibility. She'd heard of non-custodial parents kidnapping their children and taking them overseas. Was Jack capable of doing something so cruel? Years ago she'd have denied the possibility, but then she'd never have thought he'd walk out on them. How well had she known him?

She took a deep breath. 'In any case, he'll be able to see them, won't he? You're saying I could gain time by refusing but, in the end, it wouldn't make any difference, he'd still be able to see them, supervised or otherwise?'

His lips thinned. 'I'm afraid so.'

She sighed. 'I don't need this.'

'No.'

After a moment he reached for her hand and she held her breath as he entwined his fingers with hers. It looked and felt right. It was comforting. It was what she needed.

But it didn't solve her problem.

'He doesn't deserve to see them.'

Chase stayed silent.

'He abandoned them. He can't expect to waltz back into their lives and…and…' She bit her lip as her words trailed off. She didn't even know what she'd intended to say. She just knew she was angry. And scared.

Chase squeezed her hand. 'We'll go to court if that's what you want. We'll fight him.'

We?

She looked at Chase. She gazed into his eyes for an endless moment and her heart filled her throat. She could fall in love with him.

Easily.

If she hadn't already.

'Is that what you want, Regan?' he asked as if he'd read her thoughts.

Her eyes widened, then she remembered. Court. Jack. She had to think about going to court. After drawing in a long breath she said, 'I need to give it some thought.'

He nodded and gestured at her plate. 'Do you want anything else?'

She shook her head.

'Then let's go home.'

Regan didn't correct his mistake. It was *his* home, not hers. Not theirs. But tonight it was the only place she wanted to go.

And on the way to the car it seemed only natural when he held out his hand and she slipped hers into it. His long fingers curled around hers as if they were made for the purpose.

The drive home was quiet and once they were inside the house Chase glanced at Regan with concern. She frowned as she sat down, preoccupied with thoughts of her ex-husband.

Damn him.

He hated that guy for making her unhappy again. It was bad enough that he'd hurt her so badly before Chase knew her, but to come back now…

He poured two glasses of wine and carried them across the room. As he stood looking down at Regan, he thought that nobody would know she had such turmoil going on inside. She put on a good front. But he'd learned to know *her*. And he knew that inside she was a complicated mix of emotions and needs.

Complicated.

The word should have scared the life out of him but,

strangely, it didn't. The simple life he'd led with Phoebe before they'd met Regan and the boys no longer appealed to him.

He still thought about Larissa, but the feeling was more distant than he'd ever known it, more like a treasured memory. Whereas Regan was right there, within reach. And it was wanting *her* that made him ache now.

'I don't think I'll have any more wine, actually. I've had more than enough.' She stood as she spoke. 'I think I'll go straight to bed. It's been quite a day.'

'Sure.' He turned back to the kitchen and emptied both glasses into the sink. 'Regan, before you go…'

She stopped at the door and looked back, waiting.

He moved towards her. 'I want you to know…' He paused. Where to start? He wanted her to know that he was hurting for her. That he would do anything he could to help her. That he wanted her in his life…for ever.

But he couldn't get the words out. They'd agreed to be friends.

He'd promised.

So, instead, he lifted his hand and stroked her hair—just as he would do if Phoebe were in pain.

Her eyes closed. As his hand reached her jaw, she turned her face into it and pressed her lips to his palm.

He stilled. The sensation of her soft, warm lips on his skin sent panic screaming through him. He struggled against the need to kiss her, to hold her.

But, even as he fought the desire, she swayed towards him. 'Chase?'

He started, finding his hand still in mid-air and dropping it to his side. 'Yes?' he croaked.

'Don't you want to kiss me?'

'Of course I do,' he said, his voice low and sincere. 'But I said I wouldn't. I promised.'

'You said you wouldn't do anything to spoil what we have,' she corrected. 'That's not the same at all.'

'But it's what I meant.'

'Chase…'

He hesitated a moment longer, his eyes probing hers and, when he was certain that she was saying what he thought she was saying, he dipped his head and tasted her, little by little, nudging her soft lips with his until, with a groan, he closed his mouth over hers and pulled her close.

She opened to him, parted her lips and welcomed his deeper kiss. Triumph and desire flooded through him as he savoured the warm intimacy of her mouth. It was like nothing he'd known before. Her heady taste was all her own.

She'd linked her hands around his neck and they felt so right there, so natural. His own hands slid down her body and dragged her closer.

For one mind-blowing moment, she pressed her body against his…and then it was over. She eased her mouth away, moved her hands to his shoulders and put a little space between them.

She was breathing deeply. He smiled and traced her cheekbones with his fingertips. 'I can honestly say I've never enjoyed kissing anyone so much.'

'Really?'

He nodded as his fingers reached her mouth and he outlined it slowly. 'You have the most beautiful, softest lips. I think I've wanted to kiss them since I first saw your lovely face. Of course, I didn't realise it then.'

She caught his finger between her teeth and flicked her tongue over the tip. A tremor ran through him.

'You're a very sexy woman, Regan.'

She grinned, letting go of his finger. 'Nobody has ever called me sexy before.'

He gave a grunt of disbelief, then pressed his lips to the top of her head. 'So sexy. And I want you.'

Holding her close, he felt a tremor run through her body at his words. A second ticked by, then another. Finally she tipped back her head and gave him a direct look.

'I want you, too.'

Every muscle in his body tightened. He stared. 'Regan,' he whispered, 'are you serious?'

She nodded. 'And we do have the house to ourselves tonight.'

He groaned. 'We do. All night.'

The smile she gave him nearly blew his mind. It definitely took his breath away. He had no choice but to kiss her again. Hungrily this time, and with all the need he'd kept under control since he'd met her.

Regan woke up in Chase's bed and the first thing she saw when she opened her eyes was a photograph of Larissa. Every reason she'd had for not wanting this came rushing back, wrecking what should have been a beautiful morning.

Chase wasn't over Larissa. She didn't need to see a picture at his bedside to know that. Nothing had changed except that she'd thrown herself at him and they'd ended up in bed. She'd let herself be carried away by the possibility of fulfilling her physical need and had conveniently forgotten about the emotional pain she was opening herself up to.

She stared at the gorgeous face in the frame and recalled Chase's words. Petite and perfect, he'd said, and he was spot on. She had the face of an angel, hair a shade deeper than Phoebe's and a figure that made Regan feel like a lumbering, oversized frump.

No wonder he couldn't forget her. Add the fact that she had been bubbly and vivacious, and Regan knew she'd never usurp Larissa from Chase's heart.

Which left her exactly where she'd been before they'd slept together. Risking heartbreak.

If it was just her…if she didn't have to think about the boys, then maybe…maybe she could have gone along for the ride. As much as she didn't want to go through a second broken heart, it might have been worth the risk. But she *did* have to think about the boys. They came first and always would.

The pillow was wet, she realised. Her silent tears had soaked it. As carefully as possible, she slid from the bed and left the room without looking at the sleeping Chase. She didn't want to see what she was leaving behind.

When Chase awoke it was broad daylight and he felt great. He rolled over, reaching for Regan, but she'd gone. He clamped down on the disappointment that speared through him. The weekend wasn't over yet and this was only the beginning. There was no rush.

As for the day ahead, he had some ideas on how they could spend it and he couldn't wait to run them past Regan. He'd have to hurry if they were going to have time to talk them over before the kids returned.

This thought got him out of bed pretty quickly and, as he crossed the passage to the bathroom, he heard movement from Regan's room. The door was ajar and he doubled back to lean against the doorframe. 'Morning.'

His smile faded as he saw what she was doing. Packing. His spine prickled a warning and he lifted his gaze to her face in time to see her lips tremble. The stark unhappiness in her eyes made his insides twist in dread.

He pushed his hand through his uncombed hair. 'Tell me you're moving your things into my room,' he said.

She shook her head.

'You're leaving?'

His question hung in the air for a long moment and he already knew the answer by the time she nodded.

'This time it's for good. I won't be coming back again.'

He stood his ground without wavering, but inside he was reeling. 'But last night—'

'What happened last night was a mistake. I'd had too much wine and—'

'Don't tell me you didn't know what you were doing. I did not take advantage of you, Regan.' He clenched his fists in denial.

'No.' She looked away, screwed her sexy red skirt into a ball and shoved it into the bag. 'You're right. I *wanted* you.'

He frowned. 'So what's this about?' He waved a hand at her bag on the bed.

She dropped her hairdryer into the bag on top of her clothes. 'It's about us not wanting a relationship.'

'I've changed my mind.'

She froze. After a long moment she turned to face him and he saw her wide eyes linger on his bare chest before she raised them to his face. 'What about Larissa?'

He winced. But it wasn't as if he hadn't asked himself the same question, so he knew what he had to say. 'Larissa was my first love. I'll always cherish my memories of our time together. But she would want me to move on. I'm ready to move on.'

'Just like that.'

'No, Regan.' He pushed a hand through his hair again. 'You know this is a huge step for me. If anyone knows it, you do. This hasn't been a quick or an easy decision.'

She looked away. 'I know. I'm sorry. But the fact remains that I don't want to get involved with you. I *can't* get involved with you.'

'Why not?'

She looked him straight in the eye. 'Because I'd always be waiting for you to leave me.'

'*Regan.*' He straightened, but thought better of entering the room. *Keep away* vibes were rolling off her. 'I would never hurt you. Nor would I hurt Will and Cory. You can *trust* me.'

She looked up, her eyes glassy with tears. 'That's what Jack said.' Her tongue dragged across her lips. 'I don't want to make the same mistake twice.' Blinking, she went back to her packing.

Chase folded his arms across his chest. He decided not to respond to her words. He wasn't happy about being compared with that jerk of an ex-husband. He wasn't happy about any of this.

'Have you decided what you're going to do about his letter?'

She shrugged. 'If he's going to be able to see them anyway, I might as well keep our dealings amicable for the boys' sake. Or try to, anyway. I'll agree to him seeing them as long as I'm there, too.'

Chase nodded, his lips tight. 'I think that's wise.' He hesitated. 'And if he wants to come back?'

Her eyes widened. 'Come back? To me?' She gave her head an emphatic shake. 'That is not going to happen. No way.'

Well, that was something, though it did nothing to ease the pain of her leaving.

After zipping up the bag, she said, 'I think I'll go and hurry up the boys. No point in hanging around.'

Apart from the slight wobble in her voice, she could have been making a comment on the weather. How did she do that? Maybe he'd read her all wrong. Maybe she wasn't even halfway in love with him.

'No, there's no point in hanging around,' he said gruffly. 'The sooner you leave, the better.'

CHAPTER ELEVEN

REGAN sat heavily on the bed as Chase spun on his heel and left her in stunned silence, her heart hammering hard against her ribcage.

For the first time in her life she wished she didn't think so much. If she were more spontaneous, more happy-go-lucky…like Larissa…

But no. She told herself it would have been worse, much worse if she'd let a real relationship develop before the pain came. If she'd let the children see them together as a couple. If she'd allowed them to think of themselves as a family.

His words had pierced her, but she knew he'd only uttered them in retaliation, because she'd hurt him. She hadn't wanted to; he certainly didn't deserve any more pain after what he'd been through with Larissa, but this was something she had to do.

She knew she was doing the right thing for her children, and it was this certainty that gave her the strength to go through with it.

Jack had destroyed her ability to trust. Chase had rebuilt it. If he made a commitment to her, he would never break it. She understood that much. But she didn't want a commitment from a man who appeared to be still in love with another woman.

Dragging a breath deep into her lungs, she steeled herself to go and tell the children that they were leaving.

'Do we have to go home, Mum?'

Regan's throat squeezed shut at Will's dejected tone. She gave herself a moment to find her voice by kicking the nearest tyre to see if it needed air. She wouldn't have known the difference if it did.

'School starts on Monday, Will, so yes, I'm afraid we do.'

'Why can't we stay till tomorrow?'

'We have things to do. Uniforms to get ready. You want to look like everyone else when you start back, don't you?'

Will nodded and climbed reluctantly into the back of the car.

Cory swapped model trucks with Phoebe and ran around to his side of the car. 'Don't lose it,' he called to her.

Regan squatted and gathered Phoebe close for a cuddle.

'Look what Cory gave me,' she said with pride. 'His best truck.'

'He must like you a lot.' Regan's voice cracked on the last word and she buried her face in the little girl's hair while she fought for control.

Phoebe nodded. 'I like him, too. And Will. And you.'

Regan hugged her tight. 'Oh, I like you, too, sweetie. You're my favourite girl.'

After a long moment she released Phoebe and stood. Chase had said a breezy goodbye to the boys and was now leaning against the wall of the house, arms folded and face closed.

'We'll be off, then. Thank you for…everything.'

He nodded.

'I'm sorry.'

A muscle in his jaw jumped and there was a flash of raw pain in his eyes. Then it was replaced by the blank look again as he said, 'Take care.' His emotionless voice chilled her.

The tension between them grew and when she tried to say goodbye her throat was too tight. Feeling as though her breath had been cut off, she gave him a single nod and stepped into the car. She couldn't look at Chase again if she was going to hold back the tears that burned at the backs of her eyes. Reversing into the sand-strewn road, she drove off without another glance his way.

That night Chase gazed down at his daughter as she snuggled into her favourite sleeping position, curled around her teddy bear.

'Are Regan and Will and Cory coming back tomorrow, Daddy?'

'No, I told you, Sweetpea. It might be a while before we see them again.'

He couldn't bring himself to say *never*. His darling daughter had already had one *never* to accept. She'd never know a mother's love. He wasn't going to tell her that the people she'd grown so attached to had gone from her life as well.

Phoebe heaved a big sigh for a little girl and he dropped a kiss on her cheek before retreating from the room. As he closed the door, he flashed back to that morning and leaving the same room in very different circumstances. Thinking about it now, he could hardly believe he'd let it happen.

Why hadn't he argued with Regan? Made her see sense? If he'd thought she'd loved him as much as he'd discovered he loved her, he would have tried, at the very least. He knew she was running scared, but he also knew she cared about him. Last night had been...incredible. It couldn't have been so good if she weren't at least a little bit in love with him.

But he wanted her to be more than a little bit in love; he wanted the whole damned thing. If he couldn't have that...well, perhaps it was better this way.

And if he kept telling himself that, he might just start to believe it.

Regan had arranged for Jack to come to the house. She'd deliberated over this decision long and hard and had resolved that the advantages of being on her own territory would outweigh the pain of memories of them living there together. Hopefully.

When the doorbell rang she walked to the door with stiff, jerky steps. The man she invited into the house was definitely Jack but...different.

He wasn't as tall as she remembered. Not as tall as...

She stomped on that thought before it could develop.

And was that the beginning of a pot-belly pushing at the shirt fabric above his waistband?

She ushered him into the lounge and he perched on the edge of a sofa.

'You look wonderful, Regan.'

Raising an eyebrow at him, she went to fetch the boys from their room. He didn't have the right to comment on her looks, good or bad. But the surprising thing was that her stomach hadn't fluttered when he'd said it. There'd been no warm glow as a result of his words. And his voice...whiney was the word that came to mind.

The boys were polite, but they made it clear whose side they were on by sticking close to her and looking to her for guidance before answering Jack's questions.

She'd been worried that they'd beg him to move in with them. She'd tried to gently warn them that this wouldn't happen, had thought she might have been too gentle, but it seemed she needn't have been concerned about that.

Perhaps leaving the three of them alone for a few moments might help.

'Would you like a coffee, Jack?'

'Giacomo.'

'Sorry?'

'I prefer to be called Giacomo now. It's more…' He waved a hand in the air. 'Less boring.'

'Is that right?' If she had hackles, they would have risen. Was he implying that life with her had been boring? Quite likely. Gritting her teeth, she said, 'Well, was that a yes or a no, *Giacomo*?'

'Do you have an espresso machine?'

She did, actually. 'No, sorry.'

'Then I won't, thank you. Will and Cory, I have gifts for you.'

The boys' heads turned towards him as he unzipped a small leather bag—designer, she noted—and took out two of the latest portable game consoles. Great. Just what they needed—something to discourage them from healthy exercise.

Cory thanked his father politely and retreated to an armchair to play with it.

Will amazed her by declining to take it.

'Don't you like these things?' Giacomo asked.

'Yes, but Mum doesn't want us to have them.'

'Oh?' Jack looked at her, bewildered.

She shrugged. 'I prefer them to play outside.'

'We do when we're at Leo Bay,' Will said.

Her voice quivered as she said, 'Just take it, Will, and thank your father.'

'So what have you been doing for the last few years, Regan?'

She gaped. What did he think she'd been doing? 'In case you've forgotten, I had a business to rescue from imminent ruin.'

He frowned. 'I thought you'd sell it.'

She snorted. 'There wasn't much to sell by the time you'd finished with it.'

Spreading his hands in a gesture she remembered she used to hate, he said, 'I did my best.'

She bit back her angry retort. It was true. Jack—*Giacomo*—had done his best and it wasn't his fault that his best fell well short of good enough. Same with their marriage. She should have known better than to expect more from him.

'What about you?' she said instead. 'What have you been doing?'

This was a subject he could do justice to and he chattered on for several minutes about his adventures on board his friend's yacht, as well as several failed business start-ups. He didn't seem embarrassed about discussing these fiascos; it was as if he saw them as a natural part of life. She, on the other hand, would have been mortified by even one failure.

After a stilted conversation with the boys about school, Jack stood to leave. 'I'm happy that you didn't cause any difficulty about this meeting, Regan.'

Now that it had happened, she could hardly believe all the angst she'd gone through in choosing her response. She shrugged. 'Are you planning to come again?'

'Well, I'm sailing to New Zealand next week. Auckland. I could come again when I return in a month or so.'

She nodded. 'As long as you give me prior notice so that I can make sure your visit doesn't clash with our plans.'

'Of course.'

He spent some time saying goodbye to the boys and then Regan walked him to the door, where she reminded him of the dates of their sons' birthdays and suggested he make a point of contacting them on those specific days.

He admitted it was only because he'd found himself in Australia that he'd even considered meeting up with them. He hadn't made the trip with the purpose in mind, but now that he had made the effort, he promised he would maintain regular contact.

Then he left. The man she'd loved wholeheartedly. The father of her children. He walked away and she was happy to see him go, especially as he took five years of pain and anguish with him. She'd found nothing charming about his manner; if anything it was irritating and, as for his looks...well, her taste had obviously changed.

Regan wasn't one for snap decisions, but she'd made one when she'd promised to take the boys away on holiday after Jack had left. Only a couple of weeks into the school year—their teachers would love her—but it had been intended as a distraction to stop them asking about Chase and Leo Bay.

She'd wanted time to think and getting away had seemed like the only way she'd have the opportunity.

With all the excitement of the Gold Coast theme parks to occupy the boys' minds, she'd finally been able to consider her own reaction to seeing Jack again. The meeting had done something incredible. It had made her feel satisfied with everything that had happened between them and the way she'd overcome it all.

In other words, she had closure at last.

And, even better, she recognized that she'd become a stronger person as a result of the experience.

What was the saying?

What doesn't kill you makes you stronger.

Yes, she thought, in this case it was certainly true. Almost as if the divorce had been a rite of passage, helping her grow up and become a more rounded, capable person.

She had to question now why she'd ever believed she could trust Jack. It had been evident from their conversation that he was thoroughly irresponsible and incapable of sticking to anything he began.

Which had opened up a whole raft of other thoughts and questions that she'd needed time to sort through.

As Jack had no intention of taking Will and Cory away from her since they would interfere far too much with his carefree lifestyle, she was quite comfortable with the idea of him keeping in touch. He no longer had the power to hurt her and the boys might as well build some sort of relationship with him even if it wasn't the type of father-son bond they could really benefit from.

She'd come to the conclusion that she had to take fifty per cent of the blame for the end of her marriage. If she'd opened her eyes and seen Jack for what he was—immature and selfish—she wouldn't have been knocked flat by his desertion. She would have known that there was no chance of him staying with her, and she wouldn't have spent the next five years caught in a kind of fog that prevented her from trusting another person.

What she'd come to realise was that trust didn't have to be a passive thing. It was something she could choose to do with her intelligence and her strength, as well as her vulnerability.

Trusting Chase, she knew, would be a whole different ball game from trusting Jack. Chase operated from a base of honesty and integrity.

Naturally, she'd spent more time thinking about Chase than Jack and, combined with a long late-night phone chat with her closest friend, Anna, it had all led her to the belief that she needed Chase in her life. She was confused. She didn't understand how she could live with him, knowing he'd loved Larissa first and foremost, but neither did she see how she could live without him.

But would he still want her now that she'd pushed him away?

She needed to talk to him. She had to find out how he really felt about her.

As they approached home and the taxi turned into their driveway, she let out a long breath. Back to reality. She would have to see to some essential chores before she could even think about anything outside the house.

And then, amongst other things, she had to see how her new general manager had coped while she'd been away although, from what she'd learned of the guy's ability in the short time she'd worked alongside him, she had nothing to worry about.

Justin had been on the short-list of candidates sent by the employment agency and she'd hired him on impulse.

Instinct had told her he was more than capable of running the business for her, leaving her free to think about expansion or other options for growing the business when she was ready. For the time being, though, she didn't plan any major changes. She wanted to spend her time just being a mum.

'Mum, are we taking Phoebe's present to her?' Cory asked as he climbed into the car the next day.

Regan winced as she closed the door. Ostensibly, yes, they were on their way to Leo Bay to drop off the gift that Cory had insisted on buying with his pocket money. A giant inflatable shark—a ride-on water toy. But that was a big fat excuse. She just had to see Chase. She couldn't wait till the boys were at school. One more day was one day too long.

'Yes, darling,' she said as she got into the car and slipped on her sunglasses. Excitement bubbled in her veins with anticipation at seeing him again. But she knew she'd have to steel herself for the possibility that he might not be so pleased. She'd hurt him badly. She couldn't expect him to celebrate at the sight of her.

At the end of the journey it was clear that there would be no celebrating, full stop. The house at Leo Bay appeared to be closed up. Not just empty, not locked up for the day, but abandoned.

Regan couldn't understand it. With dismay she noted that there were no fishing rods on the veranda, no sand-caked shoes piled by the front door. No dog's bowl. Nothing to show that the house was occupied at all.

'Where are they, Mum?'

She swallowed past the giant lump in her throat. 'I don't know, Will.'

'At Jan's house?'

'No, they're not.' Jan's voice made Regan swing around.

'Hi,' she said with a puzzled smile.

'Hi, Regan.' Jan grinned at the boys. 'Hi, Will, Cory. How've you been?'

'Good. We've been on holiday,' Will said.

'To the Gold Coast,' Cory added.

'Oh, wow. Lucky you. I bet you had a great time.'

'We did and we bought a present for Phoebe.'

Jan nodded and looked up to meet Regan's eyes. 'They don't live here any more.'

Regan sucked a breath through her teeth. She couldn't imagine Chase leaving this lovely house, this idyllic location. Why? Where would they go?

'Did Chase leave a forwarding address?'

Jan glanced away, then back again. 'Not exactly.'

'I guess I can call his mobile.' With a hand on each boy's shoulder, Regan began to usher them towards the car.

'No, I'm sorry, he's cancelled it.'

Regan looked up in surprise. Had he gone into even deeper isolation? 'So I can't get in touch with him?'

'No, but I might be able to.'

'I'd be grateful if you'd try.'

'I'll tell him you have a toy for Phoebe, then?'

Regan paused before getting into the driver's seat. She sent Jan a sideways look, struggling to conceal the depth of her disappointment. 'Tell him…that I really need to talk to him.'

Jan's smile was a mixture of sympathy and sadness and Regan guessed she was missing Chase and Phoebe herself. 'Sure. I'll let him know if I speak to him.'

Regan nodded, then turned to open the car door. It was

the best she could hope for. She had no one to blame but herself for this disaster.

Jan walked off and Regan took a final look at the house.

What were they doing?

Until now, whenever she'd thought about Chase and Phoebe, she'd pictured them in this house. Knowing they weren't there made her stomach churn in anxiety and frustration.

Would she ever again find a place where she could feel as safe and protected as she had here?

But, more importantly, would she see Chase again? When Jan spoke to him would he decide she was too much trouble? Not worth the effort?

He hadn't left her a forwarding address. He obviously didn't want or expect her to contact him again.

CHAPTER TWELVE

THE next day Regan took Will and Cory to school, then dropped into the office, where she found everything under control. Despite a twinge of disappointment that she wasn't needed, she left. She knew she was being irrational when the whole reasoning for finding Justin was the freedom his efficiency would give her, but still, the business had been a big part of her life for years now.

She wandered around the supermarket for a while and then drove home, slamming on the brakes when she saw Chase's white car parked outside her house.

A car horn brought her back to earth and, holding her breath, she eased around the four-wheel drive vehicle and pulled in through the gates to park in the driveway. With her hand on the door catch, she looked in her side mirror and saw Chase step down.

He wore dark blue jeans and a white shirt over a navy T-shirt. He looked fabulous. Just the sight of him striding down the slope of her driveway sent her nerves into overload. But her feelings for him weren't based solely on this physical attraction, as intense as it was.

She hesitated for a moment longer, waiting for her breathing to slow before she swung open the door and got out. Feeling as if she'd left her stomach behind in the car, she faced him and watched the breeze ruffle his hair.

His eyes narrowed against the bright sun as he looked her over. 'Hello, Regan,' he said and his gentle voice touched her deep inside. 'I hope you're as well as you look.'

'I've been away on holiday.'

'I know. I called your office first.'

She nodded.

'Jan said you were looking for me.' His eyes met hers and she remembered why she'd liked him on sight. They were the kindest, warmest eyes she'd ever seen. And he'd turned out to be everything his eyes had promised.

'So she did know how to contact you.'

'I do still have the mobile phone. She was being tactful. She wasn't sure whether I wanted you to ring.'

'Did you?'

His jaw clenched but he ignored her question. 'She said you were looking for me. I thought you might need help.' He lifted his hands, dropped them again, then shoved them into his pockets and she realised something. He was nervous. As nervous as her.

It was nerves, not anger, that gave him such a serious, forbidding look, such an intimidating frown. A smouldering fire burst into flame and its glow filled her from the inside out.

With a mixture of courage and hope lightening the weight in her chest, she said, 'Yes, I need some help. Will you come inside so we can talk?'

He hesitated, flicked a glance at the house, then back at her. 'Okay.'

Sucking on her bottom lip, she led the way into the house. She paused at the entrance to the lounge room. Just a few weeks ago she'd talked to Jack in there. With a small shake of her head, she went on to the kitchen, her favourite room in the house. With a large, well-used table in the centre of the room, it was less formal, a little more like Chase's house. He'd be more comfortable there. And suddenly his comfort was very important. She desperately wanted the right to care about his comfort.

'Coffee?'

He nodded. 'If it's no trouble.'

'Have a seat.' She gestured at the table while she crossed to the espresso machine. 'How's Phoebe?'

'She's fine. She's at kindergarten.'

Shock jolted her round to face him. 'What? Here in town?'

'Yes. We live here now.'

She gave a cry of surprise. 'I had no idea. I mean…' Giving herself a mental nudge, she returned to the coffee machine. 'What's happening to the house at Leo Bay? Is it up for sale?'

'No. I could never sell it.'

She looked over her shoulder at him. 'So you're just going to leave it empty?'

He pushed a hand through his hair. 'I dare say I'll use it occasionally. Later.' The look in his eyes filled in the blanks for her. She had spoiled the house for him.

Once the coffee was ready she excused herself and went to the boys' bedroom to search for Phoebe's gift. Spotting it on the floor, she grabbed it and hurried back. She stopped in the doorway. Chase hadn't seen her; he was staring out through the glass door to the garden and her stomach went into a slow roll at the sight of his profile. She loved him so much.

She must have made a sound or a movement that gave away her presence because he looked round, straight at her.

She held out the toy, still in its packaging. 'This is for Phoebe, from the Gold Coast. Sorry, it's rather tasteless, but Cory insisted.'

He examined the picture on the label as he took it from her and a small smile curved the corners of his mouth. 'Tell them thanks. She'll enjoy it.'

Regan nodded. 'I will.'

He circled the small coffee cup with his large hands. 'So what do you need help with? Is Jack causing problems? Is he going to court?'

'No.' She smiled. 'Actually, Jack isn't causing me any problems at all.'

She saw Chase's face fall and knew he'd got the wrong idea from her words. She hurried on. 'What I mean is, Jack and I have come to an understanding over the children. He's going to see them from time to time, when he's in the country, but only by prior arrangement.'

Chase tilted his head. 'How did Will and Cory take to him?'

'Okay. They're happy about seeing him, but they're not as besotted with him as I thought they would be.' She took a sip of coffee. 'I think having had the chance to know you took some of the shine off meeting him.' Her hand shook and she put her cup down in a hurry.

He stared as if weighing her words.

'How's Phoebe getting on at kindergarten?' she asked to fill the silence.

His eyes flickered around the room. 'It's her first day today. She seemed to be settling in well when I left her, learning to mix with other children.'

'I shouldn't think she'd have a problem mixing. She was great with Will and Cory right from the beginning.'

'Yes.' He stared down at his coffee, then, frowning, looked back up at her. 'After seeing her with the boys, it was too sad to watch her all alone again.' He swallowed. 'I finally had to accept that the isolation of Leo Bay wasn't good for her. She needs company, children to play with.'

Regan's throat squeezed shut. She hadn't thought of the effect on Phoebe of their separation. But he was right. It was time for her to mix with a wider group of people.

'She's better now, but she misses you and the boys a hell of a lot.'

Regan slopped coffee on to the table. She stood, fetched a cloth to wipe it, then sat down again. 'I…we miss her too,' she said, barely keeping her voice under control. 'And…I miss you, Chase.'

Strained silence filled the kitchen for a long moment. Regan felt as though her world was on pause while she waited for his reaction.

He pushed back the chair and strode to the glass door, where he stood, looking out.

'I've made some changes since I last saw you. I've been busy. I've started a legal practice here in town, specialising in environmental cases. I've been talking to the Environmental Defenders Office and it looks like I'll be doing some work with them. It's early days, of course, but I think it's going to work out.'

'I'm pleased for you,' she said, bemused. Wasn't he going to respond to what she'd said?

He turned to face her and pushed a hand through his hair. 'And I've moved house of course. In fact, I've changed my whole life. But none of it makes a damned bit of difference.'

She stared. 'To what?'

'To wanting you. Needing you.'

Her heart leapt.

She got to her feet and wrapped her arms around her body. 'I've been doing a lot of thinking. Seeing Jack made a lot of things clear that were all muddled up before.'

'Do you still love him?'

She stared at his sombre face. The air crackled between them for several seconds. 'Absolutely not. I love *you*, Chase,' she said at last, her voice a hoarse whisper.

She pressed a hand to her chest to steady her pounding heart. She could feel the heat and the tension radiating from his body in waves. The air around her seemed to buzz and tears leaked from her eyes despite her best efforts to hold them back.

And then he was there, taking her in his arms, and she melted against him in sheer relief. Chase touched her face. He used his thumb to gently sweep a stray tear from her cheek. 'I love you, Regan. But I want us to be together. Always. I want us to be a family. All five of us. Can you agree to that? Can you trust me to stay with you through the tough times? Because if you can't…'

She lifted her head and his beautiful brown eyes locked on hers, driving away the last remnants of her fear. He wasn't some juvenile infatuation; he was her friend and soulmate. 'I love you with every part of me and I trust you completely.'

She placed a hand on his chest and felt the rapid beating of his heart.

'Marry me.'

She took a moment to absorb his words. 'Even after what you went through with Larissa, you're willing to take that risk?'

His face straight, he said, 'It's a risk everyone who loves

somebody has to take. To have everything you want, you have to risk losing it.'

He took hold of her hands. 'You're worth it, Regan. You're worth any amount of risk. You made me come alive again.'

He closed his eyes for a moment. When he opened them, she thought she saw the sheen of moisture before he pulled her against him. 'Give me a chance to show you how much I love you. I'll tell you every day. I'll show you every day. Marry me.'

Enveloped by his arms and the familiar scent of him, Regan relaxed. 'I want to have it all, too. You, marriage, a family. Your love.' Her hands found their way around his neck. 'I thought you'd never be able to give me your heart.'

She stretched up. He met her lips and she sank into the comfort of his kiss.

'No couple really knows how much time they have together,' he said when they eventually eased apart. 'We don't know. All we can do is live every minute as if it's our last and that's what we're going to do. Agreed?'

She smiled against his shoulder. They both knew how lucky they were. They would make the most of every precious hour together.

'Agreed.'

EPILOGUE

CHASE watched his two gorgeous girls as Regan spread sunscreen on Phoebe's face, then plonked a hat on her head and gave her a kiss and a hug.

His chest swelled. Nowadays it was in regular danger of bursting—every time he looked at his family.

'Dad?' He started and winked at Will, who was at his side. The boys had chosen to call their father *Jack*, and him *Dad*. He still got a thrill every time he heard it.

'You caught me checking out the talent.'

'Da-ad.' Will gave him a shove.

'Sorry. But I can't help thinking your mother's the most beautiful woman on the beach.'

'She's the *only* woman on the beach.'

'In the world, then.' Chase ruffled Will's hair. 'Where's your hat? I'm not taking you fishing without a hat.'

'It's in the boat. *Every*thing's in the boat. We're just waiting for you.'

'Okay, mate. Give me a minute to say bye to your mum.'

Will groaned. 'That'll take ages. You'll be *kissing* again.'

'Too right. Go and make sure Cory's got a hat.'

He watched Will start down the beach, then walked towards Regan. God, she was beautiful. Even more so—

if that were possible—now that she'd gained a little weight thanks to the pregnancy they'd just learned about. She filled out her new swimsuit superbly.

He could hardly believe how lucky he was. He certainly had everything he could want. As far as he was concerned, their blended family was better than any man had a right to expect.

Dropping on to the blanket, he squeezed Regan's hand. 'What are you going to do while we're out on the water?'

'I'm going to read my book and watch Phoebe swim. Then, when she's had enough, we're going to Jan's. We're overdue for a chat.'

'I'm glad you two have become such good friends.'

'Me, too. You know, she's still nagging me to leave the children with her and Mike so we can have the honeymoon we missed out on.'

'Do you want to?'

She was quiet for a moment, staring out to sea. Then she shook her head. 'No way. We couldn't find anywhere to go that would be more beautiful or more romantic than right here. And one night away from the kids is more than enough.'

He caught Phoebe as she ran past him and gave her a kiss. 'You be good while I'm away fishing with the boys, okay?'

'She's always good,' Regan said as Phoebe ran off. 'She's my little angel.'

'Yeah, right.' He leaned over to place a soft kiss on her lips. 'And you're my angel, my sweetheart, my darling love.'

'Okay, okay.' She gave him a playful slap. 'I know you promised to tell me every day that you love me but this is getting to be overkill.'

'You want me to stop?'

Her startling blue eyes softened and she reached out to touch his cheek—a light touch but it sent a thrill right through him. 'No, don't stop. Ever.'

* * * * *

Look for *LAST WOLF WATCHING*
by Rhyannon Byrd—the exciting conclusion in the
BLOODRUNNERS *miniseries*
from Silhouette Nocturne.

*Follow Michaela and Brody on their fierce journey to
find the truth and face the demons from the past, as they
reach the heart of the battle between the Runners and
the rogues.*

Here is a sneak preview of book three,
LAST WOLF WATCHING.

Michaela squinted, struggling to see through the impenetrable darkness. Everyone looked toward the Elders, but she knew Brody Carter still watched her. Michaela could feel the power of his gaze. Its heat. Its strength. And something that felt strangely like anger, though he had no reason to have any emotion toward her. Strangers from different worlds, brought together beneath the heavy silver moon on a night made for hell itself. That was their only connection.

The second she finished that thought, she knew it was a lie. But she couldn't deal with it now. Not tonight. Not when her whole world balanced on the edge of destruction.

Willing her backbone to keep her upright, Michaela Doucet focused on the towering blaze of a roaring bonfire that rose from the far side of the clearing, its orange flames burning with maniacal zeal against the inky black curtain of the night. Many of the Lycans had already shifted into their preternatural shapes, their fur-covered bodies standing like monstrous shadows at the edges of the forest as they waited with restless expectancy for her brother.

Her nineteen-year-old brother, Max, had been attacked by a rogue werewolf—a Lycan who preyed upon humans for food. Max had been bitten in the attack, which meant he was no longer human, but a breed of creature that existed between the two worlds of man and beast, much like the Bloodrunners themselves.

The Elders parted, and two hulking shapes emerged from the trees. In their wolf forms, the Lycans stood over seven feet tall, their legs bent at an odd angle as they stalked forward. They each held a thick chain that had been wound around their inside wrists, the twin lengths leading back into the shadows. The Lycans had taken no more than a few steps when they jerked on the chains, and her brother appeared.

Bound like an animal.

Biting at her trembling lower lip, she glanced left, then right, surprised to see that others had joined her. Now the Bloodrunners and their family and friends stood as a united force against the Silvercrest pack, which had yet to accept the fact that something sinister was eating away at its foundation—something that would rip down the protective walls that separated their world from the humans'. It occurred to Michaela that loyalties were being announced tonight—a separation made between those who would stand with the Runners in their fight against the rogues and those who blindly supported the pack's refusal to face reality. But all she could focus on was her brother. Max looked so hurt…so terrified.

"Leave him alone," she screamed, her soft-soled, black satin slip-ons struggling for purchase in the damp earth as she rushed toward Max, only to find herself lifted off the ground when a hard, heavily muscled arm clamped around her waist from behind, pulling her clear off her feet. "Damn it, let me down!" she snarled, unable to take her eyes off her brother as the golden-eyed Lycan kicked him.

Mindless with heartache and rage, Michaela clawed at

the arm holding her, kicking her heels against whatever part of her captor's legs she could reach. "Stop it," a deep, husky voice grunted in her ear. "You're not helping him by losing it. I give you my word he'll survive the ceremony, but you have to keep it together."

"Nooooo!" she screamed, too hysterical to listen to reason. "You're monsters! All of you! Look what you've done to him! How dare you! *How dare you!"*

The arm tightened with a powerful flex of muscle, cinching her waist. Her breath sucked in on a sharp, wailing gasp.

"Shut up before you get both yourself and your brother killed. I will *not* let that happen. Do you understand me?" her captor growled, shaking her so hard that her teeth clicked together. "Do you understand me, Doucet?"

"Damn it," she cried, stricken as she watched one of the guards grab Max by his hair. Around them Lycans huffed and growled as they watched the spectacle, while others outright howled for the show to begin.

"That's enough!" the voice seethed in her ear. "They'll tear you apart before you even reach him, and I'll be damned if I'm going to stand here and watch you die."

Suddenly, through the haze of fear and agony and outrage in her mind, she finally recognized who'd caught her. *Brody.*

He held her in his arms, her body locked against his powerful form, her back to the burning heat of his chest. A low, keening sound of anguish tore through her, and her head dropped forward as hoarse sobs of pain ripped from her throat. "Let me go. I have to help him. *Please*," she begged brokenly, knowing only that she needed to get to Max. "Let me go, Brody."

He muttered something against her hair, his breath warm against her scalp, and Michaela could have sworn it was a single word…. But she must have heard wrong. She was too upset. Too furious. Too terrified. She must be out of her mind.

Because it sounded as if he'd quietly snarled the word *never*.

nocturne™

THE FINAL INSTALLMENT OF
THE BLOODRUNNERS TRILOGY

Last Wolf Watching

Runner Brody Carter has found his match in
Michaela Doucet, a human with unusual psychic powers.
When Michaela's brother is threatened, Brody becomes
her protector, and suddenly not only has to protect her
from her enemies but also from himself....

LOOK FOR
LAST WOLF WATCHING
BY
RHYANNON
BYRD

Available May 2008 wherever you buy books.

Dramatic and Sensual Tales of Paranormal Romance

www.eHarlequin.com   SN61786

HARLEQUIN® Romance®

Western Weddings

Jason Welborn was convinced that his business partner's daughter, Jenny, had come to claim her share in the business. But Jenny seemed determined to win him over, and the more he tried to push her away, the more feisty Jenny's response. Slowly but surely she was starting to get under Jason's skin....

Look for

Coming Home to the Cattleman

by

JUDY CHRISTENBERRY

Available May wherever you buy books.

HARLEQUIN®
Live the emotion™
www.eHarlequin.com

HRI7511

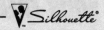

SPECIAL EDITION™

THE WILDER FAMILY
Healing Hearts in Walnut River

Social worker Isobel Suarez was proud to work at Walnut River General Hospital, so when Neil Kane showed up from the attorney general's office to investigate insurance fraud, she was up in arms. Until she melted in his arms, and things got very tricky...

Look for

HER MR. RIGHT?

by

KAREN ROSE SMITH

Available May wherever books are sold.

REQUEST YOUR FREE BOOKS!

2 FREE NOVELS PLUS 2
FREE GIFTS!

HARLEQUIN ROMANCE®

From the Heart, For the Heart

YES! Please send me 2 FREE Harlequin Romance® novels and my 2 FREE gifts (gifts are worth about $10). After receiving them, if I don't wish to receive any more books, I can return the shipping statement marked "cancel". If I don't cancel, I will receive 4 brand-new novels every month and be billed just $3.32 per book in the U.S. or $3.80 per book in Canada, plus 25¢ shipping and handling per book and applicable taxes, if any*. That's a savings of over 15% off the cover price! I understand that accepting the 2 free books and gifts places me under no obligation to buy anything. I can always return a shipment and cancel at any time. Even if I never buy another book, the two free books and gifts are mine to keep forever.

114 HDN ERQW   314 HDN ERQ9

Name	(PLEASE PRINT)	
Address		Apt. #
City	State/Prov.	Zip/Postal Code

Signature (if under 18, a parent or guardian must sign)

Mail to the **Harlequin Reader Service:**
IN U.S.A.: P.O. Box 1867, Buffalo, NY 14240-1867
IN CANADA: P.O. Box 609, Fort Erie, Ontario L2A 5X3

Not valid to current subscribers of Harlequin Romance books.

Want to try two free books from another line?
Call 1-800-873-8635 or visit www.morefreebooks.com.

* Terms and prices subject to change without notice. N.Y. residents add applicable sales tax. Canadian residents will be charged applicable provincial taxes and GST. This offer is limited to one order per household. All orders subject to approval. Credit or debit balances in a customer's account(s) may be offset by any other outstanding balance owed by or to the customer. Please allow 4 to 6 weeks for delivery. Offer available while quantities last.

Your Privacy: Harlequin Books is committed to protecting your privacy. Our Privacy Policy is available online at www.eHarlequin.com or upon request from the Reader Service. From time to time we make our lists of customers available to reputable third parties who may have a product or service of interest to you. If you would prefer we not share your name and address, please check here. ☐

HR08

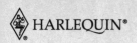

HARLEQUIN®

American ★ Romance®

Three Boys and a Baby

When Ella Garvey's eight-year-old twins and
their best friend, Dillon, discover an abandoned
baby girl, they fear she will be put in jail—
or worse! They decide to take matters into their
own hands and run away. Luckily the outlaws are
found quickly…and Ella finds a second chance
at love—with Dillon's dad, Jackson.

LOOK FOR

Three Boys and a Baby

BY

LAURA MARIE ALTOM

*Available May
wherever you buy books.*

LOVE, HOME & HAPPINESS

Coming Next Month

It's raining men this month at Harlequin Romance®, with a rancher, an Italian playboy, a sheikh boss, a Boston society heir, an entrepreneur to the rescue and a single dad to melt your heart!

#4021 COMING HOME TO THE CATTLEMAN Judy Christenberry
Western Weddings

What does home mean to you? For Jenny, it's a distant memory. But this time going home brings her into conflict with the aloof and brooding Jason, her dad's business partner, who has been less than welcoming....

#4022 THE ITALIAN PLAYBOY'S SECRET SON Rebecca Winters
Mediterranean Dads

In the second book of the spectacular duet, a terrifying crash has put race car driver Cesar Villon de Falcon in hospital, fighting for his life. Sarah has come to tell him a secret that will bring him back to life: he has a son!

#4023 THE HEIR'S CONVENIENT WIFE Myrna Mackenzie
The Wedding Planners

The series continues with more bridal fun! Photographer Regina realizes she hardly knows the man she conveniently wed. He may be strong, honorable and the heir to Boston's most distinguished business empire... but what about the man inside?

#4024 HER SHEIKH BOSS Carol Grace
Desert Brides

Duty is the most important thing in Sheikh Samir's life—an arranged marriage to a suitable woman was always his destiny. But then, on a business trip in the desert, Samir starts to see his sensible but spirited assistant Claudia in a whole new light....

#4025 WANTED: WHITE WEDDING Natasha Oakley

Do you dream of the perfect white wedding? Freya spent hours planning hers when she was young as a way to escape the troubles of home. Now she's made something of her life and all that's missing is someone to share it with—until she meets a gorgeous single dad....

#4026 HIS PREGNANT HOUSEKEEPER Caroline Anderson
Baby on Board

Wealthy architect Daniel can't turn his back on pregnant Iona, whom he finds penniless and alone in a building he is redeveloping. It's all her Cinderella fantasies come true when Daniel promises to take care of her. But can the fairy tale really last?

HRCNM0408